A BEAR CALLED

Author of over one hundred ... born in Newbury, Berkshire, ... Reading. On leaving school at the age of fourteen, he spent a year in a lawyers' office before joining the BBC as an engineer. During the war he served with both the RAF and the army, and it was in 1947, while stationed in Cairo, that he wrote his first short story. Its acceptance by London Opinion sowed the seeds of a future career, but before becoming a full-time writer he was to spend many happy and fruitful years as a BBC television cameraman.

The inspiration for his most famous creation came one snowy Christmas Eve. He was taking refuge in Selfridges when he came across a small toy bear, literally left on the shelf. It was to act as inspiration for *A Bear Called Paddington*, first published in 1958. Bears don't need much encouragement, and Paddington has since filled the pages of fourteen novels, a variety of picture books, and many other projects written for the young at heart of all ages.

Michael has twice been recognised for his services to children's literature: in 1997 he was awarded an OBE and in 2002 he was honoured in an exhibition at The National Portrait Gallery in London, celebrating a century of children's authors. He lives in London.

A Bear Called
PADDINGTON

by MICHAEL BOND

illustrated by PEGGY FORTNUM

HarperCollins *Children's Books*

First published in Great Britain by Collins in 1958
This edition published by HarperCollins *Children's Books* in 2009

HarperCollins *Children's Books* is a division of
HarperCollinsPublishers Ltd, 77–85 Fulham Palace Road,
Hammersmith, London W6 8JB

1

Visit our HarperCollins website at:
www.harpercollins.co.uk

Cover illustration adapted and coloured by Mark Burgess
from the original by Peggy Fortnum

ISBN-13: 978-0-00-731736-3

Printed and bound in Great Britain by
Clays Ltd, St Ives plc

Mixed Sources
Product group from well-managed
forests and other controlled sources
www.fsc.org Cert no. SW-COC-1806
© 1996 Forest Stewardship Council
FSC

FSC is a non-profit international organisation established to promote the
responsible management of the world's forests. Products carrying the FSC
label are independently certified to assure consumers that they come
from forests that are managed to meet the social, economic and
ecological needs of present and future generations.

Find out more about HarperCollins and the environment at
www.harpercollins.co.uk/green

CONTENTS

Chapter One

PLEASE LOOK AFTER THIS BEAR

MR AND MRS Brown first met Paddington on a railway platform. In fact, that was how he came to have such an unusual name for a bear, for Paddington was the name of the station.

The Browns were there to meet their daughter Judy, who was coming home from school for the holidays. It was a warm summer day and the station was crowded with people on their way to the seaside. Trains were humming, loudspeakers blaring, porters rushing about shouting at one another, and altogether there was so much noise that Mr Brown, who saw him first, had to tell his wife several times before she understood.

"A *bear*? On Paddington station?" Mrs Brown looked at her husband in amazement. "Don't be silly, Henry. There can't be!"

Mr Brown adjusted his glasses. "But there is," he insisted. "I distinctly saw it. Over there – near the bicycle rack. It was wearing a funny kind of hat."

Without waiting for a reply he caught hold of his wife's arm and pushed her through the crowd, round a trolley laden with chocolate and cups of tea, past a bookstall, and through a gap in a pile of suitcases towards the Lost Property Office.

"There you are," he announced triumphantly, pointing towards a dark corner, "I told you so!"

Mrs Brown followed the direction of his arm and dimly made out a small, furry object in the shadows. It seemed to be sitting on some kind of suitcase and around its neck there was a label with some writing on it. The suitcase was old and battered and on the side, in large letters, were the words WANTED ON VOYAGE.

Mrs Brown clutched at her husband. "Why, Henry," she exclaimed. "I believe you were right after all. It *is* a bear!"

She peered at it more closely. It seemed a very unusual kind of bear. It was brown in colour, a rather dirty brown, and it was wearing a most odd-looking hat, with a wide brim, just as Mr Brown had said. From beneath the brim two large, round eyes stared back at her.

Seeing that something was expected of it the bear stood up and politely raised its hat, revealing two black ears. "Good afternoon," it said, in a small, clear voice.

"Er... good afternoon," replied Mr Brown, doubtfully. There was a moment of silence.

The bear looked at them inquiringly. "Can I help you?"

Mr Brown looked rather embarrassed. "Well... no. Er... as a matter of fact, we were wondering if we could help you."

Mrs Brown bent down. "You're a very small bear," she said.

The bear puffed out its chest. "I'm a very rare sort of bear," he replied importantly. "There aren't many of us left where I come from."

"And where is that?" asked Mrs Brown.

The bear looked round carefully before replying. "Darkest Peru. I'm not really supposed to be here at all. I'm a stowaway!"

"A stowaway?" Mr Brown lowered his voice and looked anxiously over his shoulder. He almost expected to see a policeman standing behind him with a notebook and pencil, taking everything down.

"Yes," said the bear. "I emigrated, you know." A sad expression came into its eyes. "I used to live with my Aunt Lucy in Peru, but she had to go into a home for retired bears."

"You don't mean to say you've come all the way from South America by yourself?" exclaimed Mrs Brown.

The bear nodded. "Aunt Lucy always said she wanted me to emigrate when I was old enough. That's why she taught me to speak English."

"But whatever did you do for food?" asked Mr Brown. "You must be starving."

Bending down, the bear unlocked the suitcase with a small key, which it also had round its neck, and brought out an almost empty glass jar. "I ate marmalade," he said, rather proudly. "Bears like marmalade. And I lived in a lifeboat."

"But what are you going to do now?" said Mr Brown. "You can't just sit on Paddington station waiting for something to happen."

"Oh, I shall be all right... I expect." The bear bent down to do up its case again. As he did so Mrs Brown caught a glimpse of the writing on the label. It said, simply, PLEASE LOOK AFTER THIS BEAR. THANK YOU.

She turned appealingly to her husband. "Oh, Henry, what *shall* we do? We can't just leave him here. There's no knowing what might happen to him. London's such a big place when you've nowhere to go. Can't he come and stay with us for a few days?"

Mr Brown hesitated. "But Mary, dear, we can't take him... not just like that. After all..."

"After all, *what*?" Mrs Brown's voice had a firm note to it. She looked down at the bear. "He *is* rather sweet. And he'd be such company for Jonathan and Judy. Even if it's only for a little while. They'd never forgive us if they knew you'd left him here."

"It all seems highly irregular," said Mr Brown, doubtfully. "I'm sure there's a law about it." He bent down. "Would you like to come and stay with us?" he asked. "That is," he added, hastily, not wishing to offend the bear, "if you've nothing else planned."

The bear jumped and his hat nearly fell off with excitement. "Oooh, yes, please. I should like that very much. I've nowhere to go and everyone seems in such a hurry."

"Well, that's settled then," said Mrs Brown, before her husband could change his mind. "And you can have marmalade for breakfast every morning, and − " she tried hard to think of something else that bears might like.

"*Every* morning?" The bear looked as if it could hardly believe its ears. "I only had it on special occasions at home. Marmalade's very expensive in Darkest Peru."

"Then you shall have it every morning starting tomorrow," continued Mrs Brown. "And honey on Sunday."

A worried expression came over the bear's face. "Will it cost very much?" he asked. "You see, I haven't very much money."

"Of course not. We wouldn't dream of charging you anything. We shall expect you to be one of the family, shan't we, Henry?" Mrs Brown looked at her husband for support.

"Of course," said Mr Brown. "By the way," he added, "if you *are* coming home with us you'd better know our names. This is Mrs Brown and I'm Mr Brown."

The bear raised its hat politely – twice. "I haven't really got a name," he said. "Only a Peruvian one which no one can understand."

"Then we'd better give you an English one," said Mrs Brown. "It'll make things much easier." She looked round the station for inspiration. "It ought to be something special," she said thoughtfully. As she spoke an engine standing in one of the platforms gave a loud wail and a train began to move. "I know what!" she exclaimed. "We found you on Paddington station so we'll call you Paddington!"

"Paddington!" The bear repeated it several times to make sure. "It seems a very long name."

"Quite distinguished," said Mr Brown. "Yes, I like Paddington as a name. Paddington it shall be."

Mrs Brown stood up. "Good. Now, Paddington, I have to meet our little daughter, Judy, off the train. She's coming home from school. I'm sure you must be thirsty after your long journey, so you go along to the buffet with Mr Brown and he'll buy you a nice cup of tea."

Paddington licked his lips. "I'm *very* thirsty," he said. "Sea water makes you thirsty." He picked up his suitcase, pulled his hat down firmly over his head, and waved a paw politely in the direction of the buffet. "After you, Mr Brown."

"Er… thank you, Paddington," said Mr Brown.

"Now, Henry, look after him," Mrs Brown called after them. "And for goodness' sake, when you get a moment, take that label off his neck. It makes him look like a parcel. I'm sure he'll get put in a luggage van or something if a porter sees him."

The buffet was crowded when they entered but Mr Brown managed to find a table for two in a corner. By standing on a chair Paddington could just rest his paws comfortably on the glass top. He looked around with interest while Mr Brown went to fetch the tea. The sight of everyone eating reminded him of how hungry he felt. There was a half-eaten bun on the table but just as he reached out his paw a waitress came up and swept it into a pan.

"You don't want that, dearie," she said, giving him a friendly pat. "You don't know where it's been."

Paddington felt so empty he didn't really mind where it had been but he was much too polite to say anything.

"Well, Paddington," said Mr Brown, as he placed two steaming cups of tea on the table and a plate piled high with cakes. "How's that to be going on with?"

Paddington's eyes glistened. "It's very nice, thank you," he exclaimed, eyeing the tea doubtfully. "But it's rather hard drinking out of a cup. I usually get my head stuck, or else my hat falls in and makes it taste nasty."

Mr Brown hesitated. "Then you'd better give your hat to me. I'll pour the tea into a saucer for you. It's not really done in the best circles, but I'm sure no one will mind just this once."

Paddington removed his hat and laid it carefully on the table while Mr Brown poured out the tea. He looked hungrily at the cakes, in particular at a large cream-and-jam one which Mr Brown placed on a plate in front of him.

"There you are, Paddington," he said. "I'm sorry they haven't any marmalade ones, but they were the best I could get."

"I'm glad I emigrated," said Paddington, as he reached out a paw and pulled the plate nearer. "Do you think anyone would mind if I stood on the table to eat?"

Before Mr Brown could answer he had climbed up and placed his right paw firmly on the bun. It was a very large bun, the biggest and stickiest Mr Brown had been able to find, and in a matter of moments most of the inside found its way on to Paddington's whiskers. People started to nudge each other and began staring in their direction. Mr Brown wished he had chosen a plain, ordinary bun, but he wasn't very experienced in the ways of bears. He stirred his tea and looked out of the window, pretending he had tea with a bear on Paddington station every day of his life.

"Henry!" The sound of his wife's voice brought him back to earth with a start. "Henry, whatever are you doing to that poor bear? Look at him! He's covered all over with cream and jam."

Mr Brown jumped up in confusion. "He seemed rather hungry," he answered, lamely.

Mrs Brown turned to her daughter. "This is what happens when I leave your father alone for five minutes."

Judy clapped her hands excitedly. "Oh, Daddy, is he really going to stay with us?"

"If he does," said Mrs Brown, "I can see someone other than your father will have to look after him. Just look at the mess he's in!"

Paddington, who all this time had been too interested in his bun to worry about what was going on, suddenly became aware that people were talking about him. He looked up to see that Mrs Brown had been joined by a little girl, with laughing blue eyes and long, fair hair. He jumped up, meaning to raise his hat, and in his haste slipped on a patch of strawberry jam which somehow or other had found its way on to the glass table-top. For a brief moment he had a dizzy impression of everything and everyone being upside down. He waved his paws wildly in the air and then, before anyone could catch him, he somersaulted backwards and landed with a splash in his saucer of tea. He jumped up even quicker than he had sat down, because the tea was still very hot, and promptly stepped into Mr Brown's cup.

Judy threw back her head and laughed until the tears rolled down her face. "Oh, Mummy, isn't he funny!" she cried.

Paddington, who didn't think it at all funny, stood for a moment with one foot on the table and the other in Mr Brown's tea. There were large patches of white cream all over his face, and on his left ear there was a lump of strawberry jam.

"You wouldn't think," said Mrs Brown, "that anyone could get in such a state with just one bun."

Mr Brown coughed. He had just caught the

stern eye of a waitress on the other side of the counter. "Perhaps," he said, "we'd better go. I'll see if I can find a taxi." He picked up Judy's belongings and hurried outside.

Paddington stepped gingerly off the table and, with a last look at the sticky remains of his bun, climbed down on to the floor.

Judy took one of his paws. "Come along, Paddington. We'll take you home and you can have a nice hot bath. Then you can tell me all about South America. I'm sure you must have had lots of wonderful adventures."

"I have," said Paddington earnestly. "Lots. Things are always happening to me. I'm that sort of bear."

When they came out of the buffet Mr Brown had already found a taxi and he waved them across. The driver looked hard at Paddington and then at the inside of his nice, clean taxi.

"Bears is extra," he said gruffly. "Sticky bears is twice as much again."

"He can't help being sticky, driver," said Mr Brown. "He's just had a nasty accident."

The driver hesitated. "All right, 'op in. But mind

none of it comes off on me interior. I only cleaned it out this morning."

The Browns trooped obediently into the back of the taxi. Mr and Mrs Brown and Judy sat in the back, while Paddington stood on a tip-up seat behind the driver so that he could see out of the window.

The sun was shining as they drove out of the station and after the gloom and the noise everything seemed bright and cheerful. They swept past a group of people at a bus stop and Paddington waved. Several people stared and one man raised his hat in return. It was all very friendly. After weeks of sitting alone in a lifeboat there was so much to see. There were people and cars and big, red buses everywhere – it wasn't a bit like Darkest Peru.

Paddington kept one eye out of the window in case he missed anything. With his other eye he carefully examined Mr and Mrs Brown and Judy. Mr Brown was fat and jolly, with a big moustache and glasses, while Mrs Brown, who was also rather plump, looked like a larger edition of Judy.

Paddington had just decided he was going to like staying with the Browns when the glass window behind the driver shot back and a gruff voice said, "Where did you say you wanted to go?"

Mr Brown leaned forward. "Number thirty-two, Windsor Gardens."

The driver cupped his ear with one hand. "Can't 'ear you," he shouted.

Paddington tapped him on the shoulder. "Number thirty-two, Windsor Gardens," he repeated.

The taxi driver jumped at the sound of Paddington's voice and narrowly missed hitting a bus. He looked down at his shoulder and glared. "Cream!" he said, bitterly. "All over me new coat!"

Judy giggled and Mr and Mrs Brown exchanged glances. Mr Brown peered at the meter. He half expected to see a sign go up saying they had to pay another fifty pence.

"I beg your pardon," said Paddington. He bent forward and tried to rub the stain off with his other paw. Several bun crumbs and a smear of jam added themselves mysteriously to the taxi driver's coat. The driver gave Paddington a long, hard look.

Paddington raised his hat and the driver slammed the window shut again.

"Oh dear," said Mrs Brown. "We really shall have to give him a bath as soon as we get indoors. It's getting everywhere."

Paddington looked thoughtful. It wasn't so much that he didn't like baths; he really didn't mind being covered with jam and cream. It seemed a pity to wash it all off quite so soon. But before he had time to consider the matter the taxi stopped and the Browns began to climb out. Paddington picked up his suitcase and followed Judy up a flight of white steps to a big green door.

"Now you're going to meet Mrs Bird," said Judy. "She looks after us. She's a bit fierce sometimes and she grumbles a lot but she doesn't really mean it. I'm sure you'll like her."

Paddington felt his knees begin to tremble. He looked round for Mr and Mrs Brown, but they appeared to be having some sort of argument with the taxi driver. Behind the door he could hear footsteps approaching.

"I'm sure I shall like her, if you say so," he said, catching sight of his reflection on the brightly polished letterbox. "But will she like me?"

Chapter Two

A Bear in Hot Water

PADDINGTON WASN'T QUITE sure what to expect
when Mrs Bird opened the door. He was
pleasantly surprised when they were greeted by a
stout, motherly lady with grey hair and a kindly
twinkle in her eyes. When she saw Judy she raised
her hands above her head. "Goodness gracious,
you've arrived already," she said, in horror. "And

me hardly finished the washing up. I suppose you'll be wanting tea?"

"Hallo, Mrs Bird," said Judy. "It's nice to see you again. How's the rheumatism?"

"Worse than it's ever been," began Mrs Bird – then she stopped speaking and stared at Paddington. "Whatever have you got there?" she asked. "What is it?"

"It's not a *what*," said Judy. "It's a bear. His name's Paddington."

Paddington raised his hat.

"A *bear*," said Mrs Bird, doubtfully. "Well, he has good manners, I'll say that for him."

"He's going to stay with us," announced Judy. "He's emigrated from South America and he's all alone with nowhere to go."

"Going to *stay* with us?" Mrs Bird raised her arms again. "How long for?"

Judy looked round mysteriously before replying. "I don't know," she said. "It depends on *things*."

"Mercy me," exclaimed Mrs Bird. "I wish you'd told me. I haven't put clean sheets in the spare room or anything." She looked down at Paddington.

"Though judging by the state he's in perhaps that's as well."

"It's all right, Mrs Bird," said Paddington. "I think I'm going to have a bath. I had an accident with a bun."

"Oh!" Mrs Bird held the door open. "Oh, well in that case you'd best come on in. Only mind the carpet. It's just been done."

Judy took hold of Paddington's paw and squeezed. "She doesn't mind really," she whispered. "I think she rather likes you."

Paddington watched the retreating figure of Mrs Bird. "She seems a bit fierce," he said.

Mrs Bird turned. "What was that you said?"

Paddington jumped. "I… I…" he began.

"Where was it you said you'd come from? Peru?"

"That's right," said Paddington. "Darkest Peru."

"Humph!" Mrs Bird looked thoughtful for a moment. "Then I expect you like marmalade. I'd better get some more from the grocer."

"There you are! What did I tell you?" cried Judy, as the door shut behind Mrs Bird. "She *does* like you."

"Fancy her knowing I like marmalade," said Paddington.

"Mrs Bird knows everything about everything," said Judy. "Now, you'd better come upstairs with me and I'll show you your room. It used to be mine when I was small and it has lots of pictures of bears round the wall so I expect you'll feel at home." She led the way up a long flight of stairs, chattering all the time. Paddington followed closely behind, keeping carefully to the side so that he didn't have to tread on the carpet.

"That's the bathroom," said Judy. "And that's my room. And that's Jonathan's – he's my brother, and you'll meet him soon. And that's Mummy and Daddy's." She opened a door. "And this is going to be yours!"

Paddington nearly fell over with surprise when he followed her into the room. He'd never seen such a big one. There was a large bed with white sheets against one wall and several big boxes, one with a mirror on it. Judy pulled open a drawer in one of the boxes. "This is called a chest of drawers," she said. "You'll be able to keep all your things in here."

Paddington looked at the drawer and then at his suitcase. "I don't seem to have very much. That's the trouble with being small – no one ever expects you to want things."

"Then we shall have to see what we can do," said Judy, mysteriously. "I'll try and get Mummy to take you on one of her shopping expeditions." She knelt down beside him. "Let me help you to unpack."

"It's very kind of you." Paddington fumbled with the lock. "But I don't think there's much to help me with. There's a jar of marmalade – only there's hardly any left now and what there is tastes of seaweed. And my scrapbook. And some centavos – they're a sort of South American penny."

"Gosh!" said Judy. "I've never seen any of those before. Aren't they bright!"

"Oh, I keep them polished," said Paddington. "I don't *spend* them." He pulled out a tattered photograph. "And that's a picture of my Aunt Lucy. She had it taken just before she went into the home for retired bears in Lima."

"She looks very nice," said Judy. "And very

wise." Seeing that Paddington had a sad, far-away look in his eyes, she added hastily, "Well, I'm going to leave you now, so that you can have your bath and come down nice and clean. You'll find two taps, one marked hot and one marked cold. There's plenty of soap and a clean towel. Oh, and a brush so that you can scrub your back."

"It sounds very complicated," said Paddington. "Can't I just sit in a puddle or something?"

Judy laughed. "Somehow I don't think Mrs Bird would approve of that! And don't forget to wash your ears. They look awfully black."

"They're meant to be black," Paddington called indignantly, as Judy shut the door.

He climbed up on to a stool by the window and looked out. There was a large, interesting garden below, with a small pond and several trees which looked good for climbing. Beyond the trees he could see some more houses stretching away into the distance. He decided it must be wonderful living in a house like this all the time. He stayed where he was, thinking about it, until the window became steamed up and he couldn't see out any more. Then he tried writing his name on the cloudy part with his paws. He began to wish it wasn't quite so long, as he soon ran out of cloud and it was rather difficult to spell.

"All the same" – he climbed on to the dressing-table and looked at himself in the mirror – "it's a very important name. And I don't expect there are many bears in the world called Paddington!"

If he'd only known, Judy was saying exactly the same thing to Mr Brown at that very moment. The Browns were holding a council of war in the dining-room, and Mr Brown was fighting a losing battle. It had been Judy's idea in the first place to keep Paddington. In this she not only had Jonathan on her side but also her mother. Jonathan had yet to meet Paddington but the idea of having a bear in the family appealed to him. It sounded very important.

"After all, Henry," argued Mrs Brown, "you can't turn him out now. It wouldn't be right."

Mr Brown sighed. He knew when he was beaten. It wasn't that he didn't like the idea of keeping Paddington. Secretly he was just as keen as anyone. But as head of the Brown household he felt he ought to consider the matter from every angle.

"I'm sure we ought to report the matter to someone first," he said.

"I don't see why, Dad," cried Jonathan. "Besides, he might get arrested for being a stowaway if we do that."

Mrs Brown put down her knitting. "Jonathan's right, Henry. We can't let that happen. It's not as if he's done anything wrong. I'm sure he didn't harm anyone travelling in a lifeboat like that."

"Then there's the question of pocket money," said Mr Brown, weakening. "I'm not sure how much pocket money to give a bear."

"He can have a pound a week, the same as the other children," replied Mrs Brown.

Mr Brown lit his pipe carefully before replying.

"Well," he said, "we'll have to see what Mrs Bird has to say about it first, of course."

There was a triumphant chorus from the rest of the family.

"You'd better ask her then," said Mrs Brown,

when the noise had died down. "It was your idea."

Mr Brown coughed. He was a little bit afraid of Mrs Bird and he wasn't at all sure how she would take it. He was about to suggest they left it for a little while when the door opened and Mrs Bird herself came in with the tea things. She paused for a moment and looked round at the sea of expectant faces.

"I suppose," she said, "you want to tell me you've decided to keep that young Paddington."

"May we, Mrs Bird?" pleaded Judy. "Please! I'm sure he'll be very good."

"Humph!" Mrs Bird put the tray down on the table. "That remains to be seen. Different people have different ideas about being good. All the same," she hesitated at the door, "he looks the sort of bear that means well."

"Then you don't mind, Mrs Bird?" Mr Brown asked her.

Mrs Bird thought for a moment. "No. No, I don't mind at all. I've always had a soft spot for bears myself. It'll be nice to have one about the house."

"Well," gasped Mrs Brown, as the door closed. "Whoever would have thought it!"

"I expect it was because he raised his hat," said Judy. "It made a good impression. Mrs Bird likes polite people."

Mrs Brown picked up her knitting again. "I suppose someone ought to write and tell his Aunt Lucy. I'm sure she'd like to know he's safe." She turned to Judy. "Perhaps it would be a nice thought if you and Jonathan wrote."

"By the way," said Mr Brown, "come to think of it, where is Paddington? He's not still up in his room, is he?"

Judy looked up from the writing-desk, where she was searching for some notepaper. "Oh, he's all right. He's just having a bath."

"A *bath*!" Mrs Brown's face took on a worried expression. "He's rather small to be having a bath all by himself."

"Don't fuss so, Mary," grumbled Mr Brown, settling himself down in the armchair with a newspaper. "He's probably having the time of his life."

Mr Brown was fairly near the truth when he said Paddington was probably having the time of his life. Unfortunately it wasn't in quite the way he meant it. Blissfully unaware that his fate was being decided, Paddington was sitting in the middle of the bathroom floor drawing a map of South America with a tube of Mr Brown's shaving cream.

Paddington liked geography. At least, he liked *his* sort of geography, which meant seeing strange places and new people. Before he left South America on his long journey to England, his Aunt Lucy, who was a very wise old bear, had done her best to teach him all she knew. She had told him all about the places he would see on the way and she had spent many long hours reading to him about the people he would meet.

It had been a long journey, half-way round the world, and so Paddington's map occupied most of the bathroom floor and also used up most of Mr Brown's shaving cream. With the little that was left he tried writing his new name again. He had several attempts and finally decided on PADINGTUN. It looked most important.

It wasn't until a trickle of warm water landed on his nose that he realised the bath was full and was beginning to run over the side. With a sigh he climbed up on to the side of the bath, closed his eyes, held his nose with one paw, and jumped. The water was hot and soapy and much deeper than he had expected. In fact, he had to stand on tiptoe even to keep his nose above the surface.

It was then that he had a nasty shock. It's one thing getting into a bath. It's quite another getting out, especially when the water comes up to your nose and the sides are slippery and your eyes are full of soap. He couldn't even see to turn the taps off.

He tried calling out "Help", first in quite a quiet voice, then very loudly: "HELP! HELP!"

He waited for a few moments but no one came. Suddenly he had an idea. What a good thing he was still wearing his hat! He took it off and began baling out the water.

There were several holes in the hat because it was a very old one that had once belonged to his uncle, but if the water didn't get much less, at least it didn't get any more.

"That's funny," said Mr Brown, jumping up from his armchair and rubbing his forehead. "I could have sworn I felt a spot of water!"

"Don't be silly, dear. How could you?" Mrs Brown, busy with her knitting, didn't even bother to look up.

Mr Brown grunted and returned to his newspaper. He knew he had felt something, but there was no point in arguing. He looked suspiciously at the children, but both Judy and Jonathan were busy writing their letter.

"How much does it cost to send a letter to Lima?" asked Jonathan.

Judy was about to reply when another drop of water fell down from the ceiling, this time right on to the table.

"Oh, gosh!" She jumped to her feet, pulling Jonathan after her. There was an ominous wet patch right over their heads *and* right underneath the bathroom!

"Where are you going now, dear?" asked Mrs Brown.

"Oh, just upstairs to see how Paddington's getting on." Judy pushed Jonathan through the door and shut it quickly behind them.

"Crikey," said Jonathan. "What's up?"

"It's Paddington," cried Judy over her shoulder as she rushed up the stairs. "I think he's in trouble!"

She ran along the landing and banged loudly on the bathroom door. "Are you all right, Paddington?" she shouted. "May we come in?"

"HELP! HELP!" shouted Paddington. "Please come in. I think I'm going to drown!"

"Oh, Paddington." Judy leant over the side of the bath and helped Jonathan lift a dripping and very frightened Paddington on to the floor. "Oh, Paddington! Thank goodness you're all right!"

Paddington lay on his back in a pool of water. "What a good job I had my hat," he panted. "Aunt Lucy told me never to be without it."

"But why on earth didn't you pull the plug out, you silly?" said Judy.

"Oh!" Paddington looked crestfallen. "I... I never thought of that."

Jonathan looked admiringly at Paddington. "Crikey," he said. "Fancy you making all this mess. Even I've never made as much mess as this!"

Paddington sat up and looked around. The whole of the bathroom floor was covered in a sort of white foam where the hot water had landed on his map of South America. "It is a bit untidy," he admitted. "I don't really know how it got like that."

"Untidy!" Judy lifted him to his feet and wrapped a towel around him. "Paddington, we've all got a lot of work to do before we go downstairs again. If Mrs Bird sees this I don't know what she'll say."

"I do," exclaimed Jonathan. "She says it to me sometimes."

Judy began wiping the floor with a cloth. "Now just you dry yourself quickly in case you catch cold."

Paddington began rubbing himself meekly with the towel. "I must say," he remarked, looking at himself in the mirror. "I *am* a lot cleaner than I was. It doesn't look like me at all!"

Paddington *did* look much cleaner than when he had first arrived at the Browns. His fur, which was really quite light in colour and not dark brown as it had been, was standing out like a new brush, except that it was soft and silky. His nose gleamed and his ears had lost all traces of the jam and cream. He was so much cleaner that when he arrived downstairs and entered the dining-room some time later, everyone pretended not to recognise him.

"The tradesmen's entrance is at the side," said Mr Brown, from behind the paper.

Mrs Brown put down her knitting and stared at him. "I think you must have come to the wrong house," she said. "This is number thirty-two not thirty-four!"

Even Jonathan and Judy agreed there must be some mistake. Paddington began to get quite worried until they all burst out laughing and said how nice he looked now that he was brushed and combed and respectable.

They made room for him in a small armchair by the fire and Mrs Bird came in with another pot of tea and a plate of hot, buttered toast.

"Now, Paddington," said Mr Brown, when they were all settled. "Suppose you tell us all about yourself and how you came to Britain."

Paddington settled back in his armchair, wiped a smear of butter carefully from his whiskers, put his paws behind his head and stretched out his toes towards the fire. He liked an audience, especially when he was warm and the world seemed such a nice place.

"I was brought up in Darkest Peru," he began. "By my Aunt Lucy. She's the one that lives in a home for retired bears in Lima." He closed his eyes thoughtfully.

A hush fell over the room and everyone waited expectantly. After a while, when nothing happened, they began to get restless. Mr Brown coughed loudly. "It doesn't seem a very exciting story," he said, impatiently.

He reached across and poked Paddington with his pipe. "Well I never," he said. "I do believe he's fallen asleep!"

Chapter Three

PADDINGTON GOES UNDERGROUND

PADDINGTON WAS VERY surprised when he woke up
the next morning and found himself in bed. He
decided it was a nice feeling as he stretched himself
and pulled the sheets up round his head with a paw.
He reached out with his feet and found a cool spot
for his toes. One advantage of being a very small bear
in a large bed was that there was so much room.

After a few minutes he poked his head out cautiously and sniffed. There was a lovely smell of something coming under the door. It seemed to be getting nearer and nearer. There were footsteps too, coming up the stairs. As they stopped by his door there was a knock and Mrs Bird's voice called out, "Are you awake, young Paddington?"

"Only just," called out Paddington, rubbing his eyes.

The door opened. "You've had a good sleep," said Mrs Bird as she placed a tray on the bed and drew the curtains. "And you're a very privileged person to have breakfast in bed on a *weekday*!"

Paddington eyed the tray hungrily. There was half a grapefruit in a bowl, a plate of bacon and eggs, some toast, and a whole pot of marmalade, not to mention a large cup of tea. "Is all that for me?" he exclaimed.

"If you don't want it I can soon take it away again," said Mrs Bird.

"Oh, I do," said Paddington, hurriedly. "It's just that I've never seen so much breakfast before."

"Well, you'd better hurry up with it." Mrs Bird

turned in the doorway and looked back. "Because you're going on a shopping expedition this morning with Mrs Brown and Judy. And all I can say is, thank goodness I'm not going too!" She closed the door.

"Now I wonder what she means by that?" said Paddington. But he didn't worry about it for very long. There was far too much to do. It was the first time he had ever had breakfast in bed and he soon found it wasn't quite so easy as it looked. First of all he had trouble with the grapefruit. Every time he pressed it with his spoon a long stream of juice shot up and hit him in the eye, which was very painful. And all the time he was worried because the bacon and eggs were getting cold. Then there was the question of the marmalade. He wanted to leave room for the marmalade.

In the end he decided it would be much nicer if he mixed everything up on the one plate and sat on the tray to eat it.

"Oh, Paddington," said Judy when she entered the room a few minutes later and found him perched on the tray, "whatever are you doing now? Do hurry up. We're waiting for you downstairs."

Paddington looked up, an expression of bliss on his face; that part of his face which could be seen behind egg whiskers and toast crumbs. He tried to say something but all he could manage was a muffled grunting noise which sounded like IMJUSTCOMING all rolled into one.

"Really!" Judy took out her handkerchief and wiped his face. "You're the stickiest bear imaginable. And if you don't hurry up all the nice things will be gone. Mummy's going to buy you a complete new outfit from Barkridges – I heard her say so. Now, comb your fur quickly and come on down."

As she closed the door Paddington looked at the

remains of his breakfast. Most of it was gone but there was a large piece of bacon left which it seemed a pity to waste. He decided to put it into his suitcase in case he got hungry later on.

He hurried into the bathroom and rubbed his face over with some warm water. Then he combed his whiskers carefully and a few moments later, not looking perhaps as clean as he had done the evening before, but quite smart, he arrived downstairs.

"I hope you're not wearing that hat," said Mrs Brown, as she looked down at him.

"Oh, do let him, Mummy," cried Judy. "It's so... so unusual."

"It's unusual all right," said Mrs Brown. "I don't know that I've ever seen anything quite like it before. It's such a funny shape. I don't know what you'd call it."

"It's a bush hat," said Paddington, proudly. "And it saved my life."

"Saved your life?" repeated Mrs Brown. "Don't be silly. How could a hat save your life?"

Paddington was about to tell her of his adventure in the bath the evening before when he received a nudge from Judy. She shook her head. "Er… it's a long story," he said, lamely.

"Then you'd better save it for another time," said Mrs Brown. "Now come along, both of you."

Paddington picked up his suitcase and followed Mrs Brown and Judy to the front door. By the door Mrs Brown paused and sniffed.

"That's very strange," she said. "There seems to be a smell of bacon everywhere this morning. Can you smell it, Paddington?"

Paddington started. He put the suitcase guiltily behind himself and sniffed. He had several expressions which he kept for emergencies. There was his thoughtful expression, when he stared into space and rested his chin on a paw. Then there was his innocent one which wasn't really an expression at all. He decided to use this one.

"It's very strong," he said, truthfully, for he was a truthful bear. And then he added, perhaps not quite so truthfully, "I wonder where it's coming from?"

"If I were you," whispered Judy, as they walked along the road towards the tube station, "I should be more careful in future when you pack your suitcase!"

Paddington looked down. A large piece of bacon stuck out of the side of his case and was trailing on the pavement.

"Shoo!" cried Mrs Brown as a grubby-looking dog came bounding across the road. Paddington waved his suitcase. "Go away, dog," he said sternly. The dog licked its lips and Paddington glanced anxiously over his shoulder as he hurried on, keeping close behind Mrs Brown and Judy.

"Oh dear," said Mrs Brown. "I have a funny feeling about today. As if *things* are going to happen. Do you ever have that feeling, Paddington?"

Paddington considered for a moment. "Sometimes," he said vaguely as they entered the station.

At first Paddington was a little bit disappointed in the Underground. He liked the noise and the bustle and the smell of warm air which greeted him as they went inside. But he didn't think much of the ticket.

He examined carefully the piece of green cardboard which he held in his paw. "It doesn't seem much to get for eighty pence," he said. After all the lovely whirring and clanking noises the ticket machine had made it did seem disappointing. He'd expected much more for his money.

"But Paddington," Mrs Brown sighed, "you only have a ticket so that you can ride on the train. They won't let you on otherwise." She looked and sounded rather flustered. Secretly she was beginning to wish they had waited until later in the day, when it wasn't quite so crowded. There was also the peculiar business of the dogs. Not one, but six dogs of various shapes and sizes had followed them right inside. She had a funny feeling it had something to do with Paddington, but the only time she caught his eye it had such an innocent expression she felt quite upset with herself for having such thoughts.

"I suppose," she said to Paddington, as they stepped on the escalator, "we ought really to carry you. It says you're supposed to carry dogs but it doesn't say anything about bears."

Paddington didn't answer. He was following behind in a dream. Being a very short bear he couldn't easily see over the side, but when he did his eyes nearly popped out with excitement. There were people everywhere. He'd never seen so many. There were people rushing down one side and there were more people rushing up the other. Everyone seemed in a terrible hurry. As he stepped off the escalator he found himself carried away between a man with an umbrella and a lady with a large shopping bag. By the time he managed to push his way free both Mrs Brown and Judy had completely disappeared.

It was then that he saw a most surprising notice. He blinked at it several times to make sure but each time he opened his eyes it said the same thing: FOLLOW THE AMBER LIGHT TO PADDINGTON.

Paddington decided the Underground was quite the most exciting thing that had ever happened to him. He turned and trotted down the corridor, following the amber lights, until he met another crowd of people who were queuing for the 'up' escalator.

"'Ere," said the man at the top, as he examined Paddington's ticket. "What's all this? You haven't been anywhere yet."

"I know," said Paddington, unhappily. "I think I must have made a mistake at the bottom."

The man sniffed suspiciously and called across to an inspector. "There's a young bear 'ere, smelling of bacon. Says he made a mistake at the bottom."

The inspector put his thumbs under his waistcoat. "Escalators is for the benefit and convenience of passengers," he said sternly. "Not for the likes of young bears to play on. Especially in the rush hour."

"Yes, sir," said Paddington, raising his hat. "But we don't have esca... esca..."

"... lators," said the inspector, helpfully.

"... lators," said Paddington, "in Darkest Peru. I've never been on one before, so it's rather difficult."

"Darkest Peru?" said the inspector, looking most impressed. "Oh, well in that case" – he lifted up the chain which divided the 'up' and 'down' escalators – "you'd better get back down. But don't let me catch you up to any tricks again."

"Thank you very much," said Paddington gratefully, as he ducked under the chain. "It's very kind of you, I'm sure." He turned to wave goodbye, but before he could raise his hat he found himself being whisked into the depths of the Underground again.

Half-way down he was gazing with interest at the brightly coloured posters on the wall when the man standing behind poked him with his umbrella. "There's someone calling you," he said.

Paddington looked round and was just in time to see Mrs Brown and Judy pass by on their way up. They waved frantically at him and Mrs Brown called out "Stop!" several times.

Paddington turned and tried to run up the escalator, but it was going very fast, and with his short legs it was as much as he could do even to stand still. He had his head down and he didn't notice a fat man with a briefcase who was running in the opposite direction until it was too late.

There was a roar of rage from the fat man and he toppled over and grabbed at several other people. Then Paddington felt himself falling. He went bump, bump, bump all the way down before he shot off the end and finally skidded to a stop by the wall.

When he looked round everything seemed very confused. A number of people were gathered round the fat man, who was sitting on the floor rubbing his head. Away in the distance he could see Mrs Brown and Judy trying to push their way down the 'up' escalator. It was while he was watching their efforts that he saw another notice. It was in a brass case at the bottom of the escalator and it said, in big red letters: TO STOP THE ESCALATOR IN CASES OF EMERGENCY PUSH THE BUTTON.

It also said in much smaller letters, 'Penalty for Improper Use − £50'. But in his hurry Paddington did not notice this. In any case it seemed to him very much of an emergency. He swung his suitcase through the air and hit the button as hard as he could.

If there had been confusion while the escalator was moving, there was even more when it stopped. Paddington watched with surprise as everyone started running about in different directions shouting at each other. One man even began calling out "Fire!" and somewhere in the distance a bell began to ring.

He was just thinking what a lot of excitement pressing one small button could cause when a heavy hand descended on his shoulder.

"That's him!" someone shouted, pointing an accusing finger. "Saw him do it with me own eyes. As large as life!"

"Hit it with his suitcase," shouted another voice. "Ought not to be allowed!" While from the back of the crowd someone else suggested sending for the police.

Paddington began to feel frightened. He turned and looked up at the owner of the hand.

"Oh," said a stern voice. "It's you again. I might

have known." The inspector took out a notebook. "Name, please."

"Er... Paddington," said Paddington.

"I said what's your name, not where do you want to go," repeated the inspector.

"That's right," said Paddington. "That is my name."

"*Paddington!*" said the inspector, unbelievingly. "It can't be. That's the name of a station. I've never heard of a bear called Paddington before."

"It's very unusual," said Paddington. "But it's Paddington Brown, and I live at number thirty-two Windsor Gardens. And I've lost Mrs Brown and Judy."

"Oh!" The inspector wrote something in his book. "Can I see your ticket?"

"Er... I had it," said Paddington. "But I don't seem to any more."

The inspector began writing again. "Playing on the escalator. Travelling without a ticket. *Stopping* the escalator. All serious offences they are." He looked up. "What have you got to say to that, young feller me lad?"

"Well… er…" Paddington shifted uneasily and looked down at his paws.

"Have you tried looking inside your hat?" asked the inspector, not unkindly. "People often put their tickets in there."

Paddington jumped with relief. "I knew I had it somewhere," he said, thankfully, as he handed it to the inspector.

The inspector handed it back again quickly. The inside of Paddington's hat was rather sticky.

"I've never known anyone take so long not to get anywhere," he said, looking hard at Paddington. "Do you often travel on the Underground?"

"It's the first time," said Paddington.

"And the last if I have anything to do with it," said Mrs Brown as she pushed her way through the crowd.

"Is this your bear, Madam?" asked the inspector. "Because if it is, I have to inform you that he's in serious trouble." He began to read from his notebook. "As far as I can see he's broken two important regulations – probably more. I shall have to give him into custody."

"Oh dear." Mrs Brown clutched at Judy for support. "Do you *have* to? He's only small and it's his first time out in London. I'm sure he won't do it again."

"Ignorance of the law is no excuse," said the inspector, ominously. "Not in court! Persons are expected to abide by the regulations. It says so."

"In court!" Mrs Brown passed a hand nervously over her forehead. The word court always upset her. She had visions of Paddington being taken away in handcuffs and being cross-examined and all sorts of awful things.

Judy took hold of Paddington's paw and squeezed it reassuringly. Paddington looked up gratefully. He wasn't at all sure what they were talking about, but none of it sounded very nice.

"Did you say *persons* are expected to abide by the regulations?" Judy asked, firmly.

"That's right," began the inspector. "And I have my duty to do the same as everyone else."

"But it doesn't say anything about bears?" asked Judy, innocently.

"Well." The inspector scratched his head. "Not

in so many words." He looked down at Judy, then at Paddington, and then all around. The escalator had started up again and the crowd of sightseers had disappeared.

"It's all highly irregular," he said. "But..."

"Oh, thank you," said Judy. "I think you're the kindest man I've ever met! Don't *you* think so, Paddington?" Paddington nodded his head vigorously and the inspector blushed.

"I shall always travel on this Underground in future," said Paddington, politely. "I'm sure it's the nicest in all London."

The inspector opened his mouth and seemed about to say something, but he closed it again.

"Come along, children," said Mrs Brown, hastily. "If we don't hurry up we shall never get our shopping done."

From somewhere up above came the sound of dogs barking. The inspector sighed. "I can't understand it," he said. "This used to be such a well-run, respectable station. Now look at it!"

He stared after the retreating figures of Mrs Brown and Judy with Paddington bringing up the rear and then he rubbed his eyes. "That's funny," he said, more to himself. "I must be seeing things. I could have sworn that bear had some bacon sticking out of his case!" He shrugged his shoulders. There were more important things to worry about. Judging by the noise coming from the top of the escalator there was some sort of dog fight going on. It needed investigating.

Chapter Four

A SHOPPING EXPEDITION

THE MAN IN the gentlemen's outfitting department
at Barkridges held Paddington's hat at arm's length
between thumb and forefinger. He looked at it
distastefully.

"I take it the young… er, gentleman, will not be
requiring this any more, Modom?" he said.

"Oh yes, I shall," said Paddington firmly. "I've

always had that hat – ever since I was small."

"But wouldn't you like a nice new one, Paddington?" said Mrs Brown hastily, "for *best*?"

Paddington thought for a moment. "I'll have one for *worst* if you like," he said. "*That's* my best one!"

The salesman shuddered slightly and, averting his gaze, placed the offending article on the far end of the counter.

"Albert!" He beckoned to a youth who was hovering in the background. "See what we have in size $4\frac{7}{8}$." Albert began to rummage under the counter.

"And now, while we're about it," said Mrs Brown, "we'd like a nice warm coat for the winter. Something like a duffel coat with toggles so that he can do it up easily, I thought. And we'd also like a plastic raincoat for the summer."

The salesman looked at her haughtily. He wasn't very fond of bears and this one, especially, had been giving him queer looks ever since he'd mentioned his wretched hat. "Has Modom tried the bargain basement?" he began. "Something in Government Surplus…"

"No, I haven't," said Mrs Brown, hotly. "Government Surplus indeed! I've never heard of such a thing – have you, Paddington?"

"No," said Paddington, who had no idea what Government Surplus was. "*Never!*" He stared hard at the man, who looked away uneasily. Paddington had a very persistent stare when he cared to use it. It was a very powerful stare. One which his Aunt Lucy had taught him and which he kept for special occasions.

Mrs Brown pointed to a smart blue duffel coat with a red lining. "That looks the very thing," she said.

The assistant gulped. "Yes, Modom. Certainly, Modom." He beckoned to Paddington. "Come this way, sir."

Paddington followed the assistant, keeping about two feet behind him, and staring very hard. The back of the man's neck seemed to go a dull red and he fingered his collar nervously. As they passed the hat counter, Albert, who lived in constant fear of his superior, and who had been watching the events with an open mouth, gave Paddington the thumbs-up sign. Paddington waved a paw. He was beginning to enjoy himself.

He allowed the assistant to help him on with the coat and then stood admiring himself in the mirror. It was the first coat he had ever possessed. In Peru it had been very hot, and though his Aunt Lucy had made him wear a hat to prevent sunstroke, it had always been much too warm for a coat of any sort. He looked at himself in the mirror and was surprised to see not one, but a long line of bears stretching away as far as the eye could see. In fact, everywhere he looked there were bears, and they were all looking extremely smart.

"Isn't the hood a trifle large?" asked Mrs Brown, anxiously.

"Hoods are being worn large this year, Modom," said the assistant. "It's the latest fashion." He was about to add that Paddington seemed to have rather a large head anyway but he changed his mind. Bears were rather unpredictable. You never quite knew what they were thinking and this one in particular seemed to have a mind of his own.

"Do *you* like it, Paddington?" asked Mrs Brown.

Paddington gave up counting bears in the mirror and turned round to look at the back view. "I think it's the nicest coat I've ever seen," he said, after a moment's thought. Mrs Brown and the assistant heaved a sigh of relief.

"Good," said Mrs Brown. "That's settled, then. Now there's just the question of a hat and a plastic macintosh."

She walked over to the hat counter, where Albert who could still hardly take his admiring eyes off Paddington, had arranged a huge pile of hats. There were bowler hats, sun hats, trilby hats, berets, and even a very small top hat. Mrs Brown eyed them doubtfully. "It's difficult," she said, looking at Paddington. "It's largely a question of his ears. They stick out rather."

"You could cut some holes for them," said Albert.

The assistant froze him with a glance. "Cut a hole in a Barkridge's hat!" he exclaimed. "I've never heard of such a thing."

Paddington turned and stared at him. "I... er..." The assistant's voice trailed off. "I'll go and fetch my scissors," he said, in a quiet voice.

"I don't think that will be necessary at all," said Mrs Brown, hurriedly. "It's not as if he had to go to work in the city, so he doesn't want anything too smart. I think this woollen beret is very nice. The one with the pom-pom on top. The green will go well with his new coat and it'll stretch so that he can pull it down over his ears when it gets cold."

Everyone agreed that Paddington looked very smart, and while Mrs Brown looked for a plastic macintosh, he trotted off to have another look at himself in the mirror. He found the beret was a little difficult to raise as his ears kept the bottom half firmly in place. But by pulling on the pom-pom he could make it stretch quite a long way, which was almost as good. It meant, too, that he could be polite without getting his ears cold.

The assistant wanted to wrap up the duffel coat for him but after a lot of fuss it was agreed that, even though it was a warm day, he should wear it. Paddington felt very proud of himself and he was anxious to see if other people noticed.

After shaking hands with Albert, Paddington gave the assistant one more long, hard stare and the unfortunate man collapsed into a chair and began mopping his brow as Mrs Brown led the way out through the door.

Barkridges was a large shop and it even had its own escalator as well as several lifts. Mrs Brown hesitated at the door and then took Paddington's paw firmly in her hand and led him towards the lift. She'd had enough of escalators for one day.

But to Paddington everything was new, or almost everything, and he liked trying strange things. After a few seconds he decided quite definitely that he preferred riding on an escalator. They were nice and smooth. But lifts! To start with, it was full of people carrying parcels and all so busy they had not time to notice a small bear – one woman even rested her shopping bag on his head and seemed quite surprised when Paddington pushed it off. Then suddenly half of him seemed to fall away while the other half stayed where it was. Just as he had got used to that feeling the second half of him caught up again and even overtook the first half before the doors opened. It did that four times on the way down and Paddington was glad when the man in charge said it was the ground floor and Mrs Brown led him out.

She looked at him closely. "Oh dear, Paddington, you look quite pale," she said. "Are you all right?"

"I feel sick," said Paddington. "I don't like lifts. And I wish I hadn't had such a big breakfast!"

"Oh dear!" Mrs Brown looked around. Judy, who had gone off to do some shopping on her own, was nowhere to be seen. "Will you be all right sitting here for a few minutes while I go off to find Judy?" she asked.

Paddington sank down on to his case looking very mournful. Even the pom-pom on his hat seemed limp.

"I don't know whether I shall be all right," he said. "But I'll do my best."

"I'll be as quick as I can," said Mrs Brown. "Then we can take a taxi home for lunch."

Paddington groaned. "Poor Paddington," said Mrs Brown, "you must be feeling bad if you don't want any lunch." At the word lunch again, Paddington closed his eyes and gave an even louder groan. Mrs Brown tiptoed away.

Paddington kept his eyes closed for several minutes and then, as he began to feel better, he gradually became aware that every now and then a nice cool draught of air blew over his face. He opened one eye carefully to see where it was coming from and noticed for the first time that he was sitting near the main entrance to the shop. He opened his other eye and decided to investigate. If he stayed just outside the glass door he could still see Mrs Brown and Judy when they came.

And then, as he bent down to pick up his suitcase, everything suddenly went black. "Oh dear," thought Paddington, "now all the lights have gone out."

He began groping his way with outstretched

paws towards the door. He gave a push where he thought it ought to be but nothing happened. He tried moving along the wall a little way and gave another push. This time it did move. The door seemed to have a strong spring on it and he had to push hard to make it open but eventually there was a gap big enough for him to squeeze through. It clanged shut behind him and Paddington was disappointed to find it was just as dark outside as it had been in the shop. He began to wish he'd stayed where he was. He turned round and tried to find the door but it seemed to have disappeared.

He decided it might be easier if he got down on his paws and crawled. He went a little way like this and then his head came up against something hard. He tried to push it to one side with his paw and it moved slightly so he pushed again.

Suddenly, there was a noise like thunder, and before he knew where he was a whole mountain of things began to fall on him. It felt as if the whole sky had fallen in. Everything went quiet and he lay where he was for a few minutes with his eyes tightly shut, hardly daring to breathe. From a long way away he could hear voices and once or twice it sounded as if someone was banging on a window. He opened one eye carefully and was surprised to find the light had come on again. At least... Sheepishly he pushed the hood of his duffel coat up over his head. They hadn't gone out at all! His hood must have fallen over his head when he bent down inside the shop to pick up his case.

Paddington sat up and looked around to see where he was. He felt much better now. Somewhat to his astonishment, he found he was sitting in a small room in the middle of which was a great pile of tins and basins and bowls. He rubbed his eyes and stared, round-eyed, at the sight.

Behind him there was a wall with a door in it,

and in front of him there was a large window. On the other side of the window there was a large crowd of people pushing one another and pointing in his direction. Paddington decided with pleasure that they must be pointing at him. He stood up with difficulty, because it was hard standing up straight on top of a lot of tins, and pulled the pom-pom on his hat as high as it would go. A cheer went up from the crowd. Paddington gave a bow, waved several times, and then started to examine the damage all around him.

For a moment he wasn't quite sure where he was, and then it came to him. Instead of going out into the street he must have opened a door leading to one of the shop windows!

Paddington was an observant bear, and since he had arrived in London he'd noticed lots of these shop windows. They were very interesting. They always had so many things inside them to look at. Once, he'd seen a man working in one, piling tin cans and boxes on top of each other to make a pyramid. He remembered deciding at the time what a nice job it must be.

He looked round thoughtfully. "Oh dear," he said to the world in general, "I'm in trouble again." If he'd knocked all these things down, as he supposed he must have done, someone was going to be cross. In fact, lots of people were going to be cross. People weren't very good at having things explained to them and it was going to be difficult explaining how his duffel coat hood had fallen over his head.

He bent down and began to pick up the things. There were some glass shelves lying on the floor where they had fallen. It was getting warm inside the window so he took off his duffel coat and hung it carefully on a nail. Then he picked up a glass shelf and tried balancing it on top of some tins. It seemed to work so he put some more tins and a washing-up bowl on top of that. It was rather wobbly but... he stood back and examined it... yes, it looked quite nice. There was an encouraging round of applause from outside. Paddington waved a paw at the crowd and picked up another shelf.

Inside the shop, Mrs Brown was having an earnest conversation with the store detective.

"You say you left him here, Madam?" the detective was saying.

"That's right," said Mrs Brown. "He was feeling ill and I *told* him not to go away. His name's Paddington."

"Paddington." The detective wrote it carefully in his notebook. "What sort of bear is he?"

"Oh, he's sort of golden," said Mrs Brown. "He was wearing a blue duffel coat and carrying a suitcase."

"And he has black ears," said Judy. "You can't mistake him."

"Black ears," the detective repeated, licking his pencil.

"I don't expect that'll help much," said Mrs Brown. "He was wearing his beret."

The detective cupped his hand over his ear. "His *what?*" he shouted. There really was a terrible noise coming from somewhere. It seemed to be getting worse every minute. Every now and then there was a round of applause and several times he distinctly heard the sound of people cheering.

"His *beret*," shouted Mrs Brown in return.

"A green woollen one that came down over his ears. With a pom-pom."

The detective shut his notebook with a snap. The noise outside was definitely getting worse. "Pardon me," he said, sternly. "There's something strange going on that needs investigating."

Mrs Brown and Judy exchanged glances. The same thought was running through both their minds. They both said "Paddington!" and rushed after the detective. Mrs Brown clung to the detective's coat and Judy clung to Mrs Brown's as they forced their way through the crowd on the pavement. Just as they reached the window a tremendous cheer went up.

"I might have known," said Mrs Brown.

"Paddington!" exclaimed Judy.

Paddington had just reached the top of his pyramid. At least, it had started off to be a pyramid, but it wasn't really. It wasn't any particular shape at all and it was very rickety. Having placed the last tin on the top Paddington was in trouble. He wanted to get down but he couldn't. He reached out a paw and the mountain began to wobble.

Paddington clung helplessly to the tins, swaying to and fro, watched by a fascinated audience. And then, without any warning, the whole lot collapsed again, only this time Paddington was on top and not underneath. A groan of disappointment went up from the crowd.

"Best thing I've seen in years," said a man in the crowd to Mrs Brown. "Blessed if I know how they think these things up."

"Will he do it again, Mummy?" asked a small boy.

"I don't think so, dear," said his mother. "I think he's finished for the day." She pointed to the window where the detective was removing a sorry-looking Paddington. Mrs Brown hurried back to the entrance followed by Judy.

Inside the shop the detective looked at Paddington and then at his notebook. "Blue duffel coat," he said. "Green woollen beret!" He pulled the beret off. "Black ears! I know who you are," he said grimly; "you're Paddington!"

Paddington nearly fell backwards with astonishment.

"However did you know that?" he said.

"I'm a detective," said the man. "It's my job to know these things. We're always on the look-out for criminals."

"But I'm not a criminal," said Paddington hotly. "I'm a bear! Besides, I was only tidying up the window…"

"Tidying up the window," the detective spluttered. "I don't know what Mr Perkins will have to say. He only dressed it this morning."

Paddington looked round uneasily. He could see Mrs Brown and Judy hurrying towards him. In fact, there were several people coming his way, including an important-looking man in a black coat and striped trousers. They all reached him at the same time and all began talking together.

Paddington sat down on his case and watched them. There were times when it was much better to keep quiet, and this was one of them. In the end it was the important-looking man who won, because he had the loudest voice and kept on talking when everyone else had finished.

To Paddington's surprise he reached down, took

hold of his paw, and started to shake it so hard he thought it was going to drop off.

"Delighted to know you, bear," he boomed. "Delighted to know you. And congratulations."

"That's all right," said Paddington, doubtfully. He didn't know why, but the man seemed very pleased.

The man turned to Mrs Brown. "You say his name's Paddington?"

"That's right," said Mrs Brown. "And I'm sure he didn't mean any harm."

"Harm?" The man looked at Mrs Brown in amazement. "Did you say harm? My dear lady, through the action of this bear we've had the biggest crowd in years. Our telephone hasn't stopped ringing." He waved towards the entrance to the store. "And still they come!"

He placed his hand on Paddington's head. "Barkridges," he said, "Barkridges is grateful!" He waved his other hand for silence. "We would like to show our gratitude. If there is anything... anything in the store you would like...?"

Paddington's eyes gleamed. He knew just what

he wanted. He'd seen it on their way up to the outfitting department. It had been standing all by itself on a counter in the food store. The biggest one he'd ever seen. Almost as big as himself.

"Please," he said. "I'd like one of those jars of marmalade. One of the big ones."

If the manager of Barkridges felt surprised he didn't show it. He stood respectfully to one side, by the entrance to the lift.

"Marmalade it shall be," he said, pressing the button.

"I think," said Paddington, "if you don't mind, I'd rather use the stairs."

Chapter Five

PADDINGTON AND THE 'OLD MASTER'

PADDINGTON SOON SETTLED down and became one of the family. In fact, in no time at all it was difficult to imagine what life had been like without him. He made himself useful about the house and the days passed quickly. The Browns lived near the Portobello Road where there was a big market and quite often, when Mrs Brown was busy, she let him go out to do the shopping for her. Mr Brown made a shopping trolley for him – an old basket on wheels with a handle for steering it.

Paddington was a good shopper and soon became well known to all the traders in the market. He was very thorough and took the job of shopping seriously. He would press the fruit to see that it had the right degree of firmness, as Mrs Bird had shown him, and he was always on the look-out for bargains. He was a popular bear with the traders and most of them went out of their way to save the best things of the day for him.

"That bear gets more for his ten pence than anyone I know," said Mrs Bird. "I don't know how he gets away with it, really I don't. It must be the mean streak in him."

"I'm not mean," said Paddington, indignantly. "I'm just careful, that's all."

"Whatever it is," replied Mrs Bird, "you're worth your weight in gold."

Paddington took this remark very seriously, and spent a long time weighing himself on the bathroom scales. Eventually he decided to consult his friend, Mr Gruber, on the subject.

Now Paddington spent a lot of his time looking in shop windows, and of all the windows in the Portobello Road, Mr Gruber's was the best. For one thing it was nice and low so that he could look in without having to stand on tiptoe, and for another, it was full of interesting things. Old pieces of furniture, medals, pots and pans, pictures; there were so many things it was difficult to get inside the shop, and old Mr Gruber spent a lot of his time sitting in a deck-chair on the pavement. Mr Gruber, in his turn, found Paddington very interesting and soon they had become great friends. Paddington often stopped there on his way home from a shopping expedition and they spent many hours discussing South America, where Mr Gruber had been when he was a boy. Mr Gruber usually had a bun and a cup of cocoa in the morning for what he called his 'elevenses', and he had taken to sharing it with Paddington. "There's nothing like a nice chat over a bun and a cup of cocoa," he used to say, and Paddington, who liked all three, agreed with him – even though the cocoa did make his whiskers go a funny colour.

Paddington was always interested in bright things and he had consulted Mr Gruber one morning on the subject of his Peruvian centavos. He had an idea in the back of his mind that if they were worth a lot of money he could perhaps sell them and buy a present for the Browns. The one pound a week pocket-money Mr Brown gave him was nice, but by the time he had bought some buns on a Saturday morning there wasn't much left. After a great deal of consideration, Mr Gruber had advised Paddington to keep the coins. "It's not always the brightest things that fetch the most money, Mr Brown," he had said. Mr Gruber always called Paddington 'Mr Brown', and it made him feel very important.

He had taken Paddington into the back of the shop where his desk was, and from a drawer he had taken a cardboard box full of old coins. They had been rather dirty and disappointing. "See these, Mr Brown?" he had said. "These are what they call sovereigns. You wouldn't think they were very valuable to look at them, but they are. They're made of gold and they're worth fifty pounds each. That's more than one hundred pounds for an ounce. If you ever find any of those, just you bring them to me."

One day, having weighed himself carefully on the scales, Paddington hurried round to Mr Gruber, taking with him a piece of paper from his scrapbook, covered with mysterious calculations. After a big meal on a Sunday, Paddington had discovered he weighed nearly sixteen pounds. That was... he looked at his piece of paper again as he neared Mr Gruber's shop... that was nearly two hundred and sixty ounces, which meant he was worth nearly twenty six thousand pounds!

Mr Gruber listened carefully to all that Paddington had to tell him and then closed his eyes and thought for a moment. He was a kindly man, and he didn't want to disappoint Paddington.

"I've no doubt," he said at last, "that you're *worth* that. You're obviously a very valuable young bear. I know it. Mr and Mrs Brown know it. Mrs Bird knows it. But do other people?"

He looked at Paddington over his glasses. "Things aren't always what they seem in this world, Mr Brown," he said sadly.

Paddington sighed. It was very disappointing. "I wish they were," he said. "It would be nice."

"Perhaps," said Mr Gruber, mysteriously. "Perhaps. But we shouldn't have any nice surprises then, should we?"

He took Paddington into his shop and after offering him a seat disappeared for a moment. When he returned he was carrying a large picture of a boat. At least, half of it was a boat. The other half seemed to be the picture of a lady in a large hat.

"There you are," he said proudly. "That's what I mean by things not always being what they seem. I'd like your opinion on it, Mr Brown."

Paddington felt rather flattered but also puzzled. The picture didn't seem to be one thing or the other and he said so.

"Ah," said Mr Gruber, delightedly. "It isn't at the moment. But just you wait until I've cleaned it! I gave fifty pence for that picture years and years ago, when it was just a picture of a sailing ship. And what do you think? When I started to clean it the other day all the paint began to come off and I discovered there was another painting underneath." He looked around and then lowered his voice. "Nobody else knows," he whispered, "but I think the one underneath may be valuable. It may be what they call an 'old master'."

Seeing that Paddington still looked puzzled, he explained to him that in the old days, when artists ran short of money and couldn't afford any canvas to paint on, they sometimes painted on top of old pictures. And sometimes, very occasionally, they painted them on top of pictures by artists who afterwards became famous and whose pictures were worth a lot of money. But as they had been painted over, no one knew anything about them.

"It all sounds very complicated," said Paddington thoughtfully.

Mr Gruber talked for a long time about painting, which was one of his favourite subjects. But Paddington, though he was usually interested in anything Mr Gruber had to tell him, was hardly listening. Eventually, refusing Mr Gruber's offer of a second cup of cocoa, he slipped down off the chair and began making his way home. He raised his hat automatically whenever anyone said good-day to him, but there was a far-away expression in his eyes. Even the smell of buns from the bakery passed unheeded. Paddington had an idea.

When he got home he went upstairs to his room and lay on the bed for a long while staring up at the ceiling. He was up there so long that Mrs Bird became quite worried and poked her head round the door to know if he was all right.

"Quite all right, thank you," said Paddington, distantly. "I'm just thinking."

Mrs Bird closed the door and hurried downstairs to tell the others. Her news had a mixed reception. "I don't mind him *just* thinking," said Mrs Brown, with a worried expression on her face. "It's when he actually thinks *of* something that the trouble starts."

But she was in the middle of her housework and soon forgot the matter. Certainly both she and Mrs Bird were much too busy to notice the small figure of a bear creeping cautiously in the direction of Mr Brown's shed a few minutes later. Nor did they see him return armed with a bottle of Mr Brown's paint remover and a large pile of rags. Had they done so they might have had good cause to worry. And if Mrs Brown had seen him creeping on tiptoe into the drawing-room, closing the door carefully behind him, she wouldn't have had a minute's peace.

Fortunately everyone was much too busy to notice any of these things. Even more fortunately, no one came into the drawing-room for quite a long while. Because Paddington was in a mess. Things hadn't gone at all according to plan. He was beginning to wish he had listened more carefully to the things Mr Gruber had said on the subject of cleaning paintings.

To start with, even though he'd used almost half a bottle of Mr Brown's paint remover, the picture had only come off in patches. Secondly, and what was even worse, where it *had* come off there was nothing underneath. Only the white canvas. Paddington stood back and surveyed his handiwork. Originally it had been a painting of a lake, with a blue sky and several sailing boats dotted around. Now it looked like a storm at sea. All the boats had gone, the sky was a funny shade of grey, and half the lake had disappeared.

"What a good thing I found this old box of paints," he thought, as he stood back holding the end of the brush at paw's length and squinting at it as he'd once seen a real artist do. Holding a palette in his left paw, he squeezed some red paint on to it and then splodged it about with the brush. He looked nervously over his shoulder and then dabbed some of it on to the canvas.

Paddington had found the paints in a cupboard under the stairs. A whole box of them. There were reds and greens and yellows and blues. In fact, there were so many different colours it was difficult to know which to choose first.

He wiped the brush carefully on his hat and tried another colour and then another. It was all so interesting that he thought he would try a bit of each, and he very soon forgot the fact that he was supposed to be painting a picture.

In fact, it was more of a design than a picture, with lines and circles and crosses in all different colours. Even Paddington was startled when he finally stepped back to examine it. Of the original picture there was no trace at all. Rather sadly he put the tubes of paint back into the box and wrapped the picture in a canvas bag, leaning it against the wall, exactly as he'd found it. He decided reluctantly to have another try later on. Painting was fun while it lasted but it was much more difficult than it looked.

He was very silent all through dinner that evening. He was so silent that several times Mrs Brown asked him how he was, until eventually Paddington asked to be excused and went upstairs.

"I do hope he's all right, Henry," she said, after he'd gone. "He hardly touched his dinner and that's so unlike him. And he seemed to have some funny red spots all over his face."

"Crikey," said Jonathan. "Red spots! I hope he's given it to me, whatever it is, then I shan't have to go back to school!"

"Well, he's got green ones as well," said Judy. "I saw some green ones!"

"*Green* ones!" Even Mr Brown looked worried. "I wonder if he's sickening for anything? If they're not gone in the morning I'll send for the doctor."

"He was so looking forward to going to the handicrafts exhibition, too," said Mrs Brown. "It'll be a shame if he has to stay in bed."

"Do you think you'll win a prize with your painting, Dad?" asked Jonathan.

"No one will be more surprised than your father if he does," replied Mrs Brown. "He's never won a prize yet!"

"What is it, Daddy?" asked Judy. "Aren't you going to tell us?"

"It's meant to be a surprise," said Mr Brown modestly. "It took me a long time to do. It's painted from memory."

Painting was one of Mr Brown's hobbies, and once a year he entered a picture for a handicrafts exhibition which was held in Kensington, near where they lived. Several famous people came to judge the pictures and there were a number of prizes. There were also lots of other competitions, and it was a sore point with Mr Brown that he had never won anything, whereas twice Mrs Brown had won a prize in the rug-making competition.

"Anyway," he said, declaring the subject closed, "it's too late now. The man collected it this afternoon, so we shall see what we shall see."

The sun was shining the next day and the exhibition was crowded. Everyone was pleased that Paddington looked so much better. His spots had completely disappeared and he ate a large breakfast to make up for missing so much dinner the night before. Only Mrs Bird had her suspicions when she found Paddington's 'spots' on his towel in the bathroom, but she kept her thoughts to herself.

The Browns occupied the middle five seats of the front row where the judging was to take place. There was an air of great excitement. It was news to Paddington that Mr Brown actually painted and he was looking forward to seeing a picture by someone he knew.

On the platform several important-looking men with beards were bustling about talking to each other and waving their arms in the air. They appeared to be having a great deal of argument about one painting in particular.

"Henry," whispered Mrs Brown, excitedly. "I do believe they're talking about yours. I recognise the canvas bag."

Mr Brown looked puzzled. "It certainly looks like my bag," he said. "But I don't think it can be. All the canvas was stuck to the painting. Didn't you see? Just as if someone had put it inside while it was still wet. I painted mine ages ago."

Paddington sat very still and stared straight ahead, hardly daring to move. He had a strange sinking feeling in the bottom of his stomach, as if something awful was about to happen. He began to wish he hadn't washed his spots off that morning; then at least he could have stayed in bed.

Judy poked him with her elbow. "What's the matter, Paddington?" she asked. "You look most peculiar. Are you all right?"

"I don't feel ill," said Paddington in a small voice. "But I think I'm in trouble again."

"Oh dear," said Judy. "Well, keep your paws crossed. This is it!"

Paddington sat up. One of the men on the platform, the most important-looking one with the biggest beard, was speaking. And there... Paddington's knees began to tremble, there on the platform, on an easel in full view of everyone, was 'his' picture!

He was so dazed he only caught scraps of what the man was saying.

"... remarkable use of colour..."

"... very unusual..."

"... great imagination... a credit to the artist..."

And then, he almost fell off his seat with surprise. "The winner of the first prize is Mr Henry Brown of thirty-two Windsor Gardens!"

Paddington wasn't the only one who felt surprised. Mr Brown, who was being helped up on to the platform, looked as if he had just been struck by lightning. "But... but..." he stuttered, "there must be some mistake."

"Mistake?" said the man with the beard. "Nonsense, my dear sir. Your name's on the back of the canvas. You *are* Mr Brown, aren't you? Mr *Henry* Brown?"

Mr Brown looked at the painting with unbelieving eyes. "It's certainly my name on the back," he said. "It's my writing..." He left the sentence unfinished and looked down towards the audience. He had his own ideas on the subject, but it was difficult to catch Paddington's eye. It usually was when you particularly wanted to.

"I think," said Mr Brown, when the applause had died down, and he had accepted the cheque for ten pounds which the man gave him, "proud as I am, I think I would like to donate the prize to a certain home for retired bears in South America." A murmur of surprise went round the assembly but it passed over Paddington's head, though he would have been very pleased had he known its cause. He was staring hard at the painting, and in particular at the man with the large beard, who was beginning to look hot and bothered.

"I think," said Paddington, to the world in general, "they might have stood it the right way up. It's not every day a bear wins first prize in a painting competition!"

Chapter Six

A VISIT TO THE THEATRE

THE BROWNS WERE all very excited. Mr Brown had been given tickets for a box at the theatre. It was the first night of a brand new play, and the leading part was being played by the world famous actor, Sir Sealy Bloom. Even Paddington became infected with the excitement. He made several journeys to his friend, Mr Gruber, to have the theatre explained to him. Mr Gruber thought he was very lucky to be going to the first night of a new play. "All sorts of famous people will be there," he said. "I don't suppose many bears have that sort of opportunity once in a lifetime."

Mr Gruber lent Paddington several second-hand books about the theatre. He was rather a slow reader but there were lots of pictures and, in one of them, a big cut-out model of a stage which sprang up every time he opened the pages. Paddington decided that when he grew up he wanted to be an actor. He took to standing on his dressing-table and striking poses in the mirror just as he had seen them in the books.

Mrs Brown had her own thoughts on the subject. "I do hope it's a nice play," she said to Mrs Bird. "You know what Paddington's like… he does take these things so seriously."

"Oh, well," said Mrs Bird. "*I* shall sit at home and listen to the wireless in peace and quiet. But it'll be an experience for him and he does like experiences so. Besides, he's been very good lately."

"I know," said Mrs Brown. "That's what worries me!"

As it turned out, the play itself was the least of Mrs Brown's worries. Paddington was unusually silent all the way to the theatre. It was the first time he had been out after dark and the very first time he had seen the lights of London. Mr Brown pointed out all the famous landmarks as they drove past in the car, and it was a gay party of Browns that eventually trooped into the theatre.

Paddington was pleased to find it all exactly as Mr Gruber had described it to him, even down to the commissionaire who opened the door for them and saluted as they entered the foyer.

Paddington returned the salute with a wave of his paw and then sniffed. Everything was painted red and gold and the theatre had a nice, warm, friendly sort of smell. There was a slight upset at the cloakroom when he found he had to pay in order to leave his duffel coat and suitcase. The woman behind the counter turned quite nasty when Paddington asked for his things back.

She was still talking about it in a loud voice as

the attendant led them along a passage towards their seats. At the entrance to the box the attendant paused.

"Programme, sir?" she said to Paddington.

"Yes, please," said Paddington, taking five. "Thank you very much."

"And would you like coffee in the interval, sir?" she asked.

Paddington's eyes glistened. "Oh, yes, please," he said, imagining it was a kind thought on the part of the theatre. He tried to push his way past, but the attendant barred the way.

"That'll be seven pounds fifty pence," she said. "One pound each for the programmes and fifty pence each for the coffee."

Paddington looked as if he could hardly believe his ears. "Seven pounds and fifty pence?" he repeated. "*Seven pounds fifty?*"

"That's all right, Paddington," said Mr Brown, anxious to avoid another fuss. "It's my treat. You go in and sit down."

Paddington obeyed like a shot, but he gave the attendant some very queer looks while she arranged some cushions for his seat in the front row. All the same, he was pleased to see she had given him the one nearest the stage. He'd already sent a postcard to his Aunt Lucy with a carefully drawn copy of a plan of the theatre, which he'd found in one of Mr Gruber's books, and a small cross in one corner marked 'MY SEET'.

The theatre was quite full and Paddington waved to the people down below. Much to Mrs Brown's embarrassment, several of them pointed and waved back.

"I *do* wish he wouldn't be quite so friendly," she whispered to Mr Brown.

"Wouldn't you like to take off your duffel coat now?" asked Mr Brown. "It'll be cold when you go out again."

Paddington climbed up and stood on his chair. "I think perhaps I will," he said. "It's getting warm."

Judy started to help him off with it. "Mind my marmalade sandwich!" cried Paddington, as she placed it on the ledge in front of him. But it was too late. He looked round guiltily.

"Crikey!" said Jonathan. "It's fallen on someone's head!" He looked over the edge of the box. "It's that man with the bald head. He looks jolly cross."

"Oh, Paddington!" Mrs Brown looked despairingly at him. "Do you *have* to bring marmalade sandwiches to the theatre?"

"It's all right," said Paddington, cheerfully. "I've some more in the other pocket if anyone wants one. They're a bit squashed, I'm afraid, because I sat on them in the car."

"There seems to be some sort of a row going on down below," said Mr Brown, craning his head to look over the edge. "Some chap just waved his fist at me. And what's all this about marmalade sandwiches?" Mr Brown was a bit slow on the uptake sometimes.

"Nothing, dear," said Mrs Brown, hastily. She decided to let the matter drop. It was much easier in the long run.

In any case, Paddington was having a great struggle with himself over some opera glasses. He had just seen a little box in front of him marked OPERA GLASSES. TWENTY PENCE. Eventually, after a great deal of thought, he unlocked his suitcase and from a secret compartment withdrew twenty pence.

"I don't think much of these," he said, a moment later, looking through them at the audience. "Everyone looks smaller."

"You've got them the wrong way round, silly," said Jonathan.

"Well, I still don't think much of them," said Paddington, turning them round. "I wouldn't have bought them if I'd known. Still," he added, after a moment's thought, "they might come in useful next time."

Just as he began to speak the overture came to an end and the curtain rose. The scene was the living-room of a large house, and Sir Sealy Bloom, in the part of the village squire, was pacing up and down. There was a round of applause from the audience.

"You don't take them home," whispered Judy. "You have to put them back when you leave."

"WHAT!" cried Paddington, in a loud voice. Several calls of 'hush' came from the darkened theatre as Sir Sealy Bloom paused and looked pointedly in the direction of the Browns' box. "Do you mean to say..." words failed Paddington for the moment. "*Twenty pence!*" he said bitterly. "That's two buns' worth." He turned his gaze on Sir Sealy Bloom.

Sir Sealy Bloom looked rather irritable. He didn't like first nights, and this one in particular had started badly. He had a nasty feeling about it. He much preferred playing the hero, where he had the sympathy of the audience, and in this play he was the villain. Being the first night of the play, he wasn't at all sure of some of his lines. To make matters worse, he had arrived at the theatre only to discover that the prompt boy was missing and there was no one else to take his place. Then there was the disturbance in the stalls just before the curtain went up. Something to do with a marmalade sandwich, so the stage manager had said. Of course, that was all nonsense, but still, it was very disturbing. And then there was this noisy crowd in the box. He sighed to himself. It was obviously going to be one of those nights.

But if Sir Sealy Bloom's heart was not in the play, Paddington's certainly was. He soon forgot about his wasted twenty pence and devoted all his attention to the plot. He decided quite early on that he didn't like Sir Sealy Bloom and he stared at him hard through his opera glasses. He followed his every move and when, at the end of the first act, Sir Sealy, in the part of the hard-hearted father, turned his daughter out into the world without a penny, Paddington stood up on his chair and waved his programme indignantly at the stage.

Paddington was a surprising bear in many ways and he had a strong sense of right and wrong. As the curtain came down he placed his opera glasses firmly on the ledge and climbed off his seat.

"Are you enjoying it, Paddington?" asked Mr Brown.

"It's very interesting," said Paddington. He had a determined note to his voice and Mrs Brown looked at him sharply. She was beginning to recognise that tone and it worried her.

"Where are you going, dear?" she asked, as he made for the door of the box.

"Oh, just for a walk," said Paddington, vaguely.

"Well, don't be too long," she called, as the door closed behind him. "You don't want to miss any of the second act."

"Oh, don't fuss, Mary," said Mr Brown. "I expect he just wants to stretch his legs or something. He's probably gone out to the cloakroom."

But at that moment Paddington was going, not in the direction of the cloakroom, but towards a door leading to the back of the theatre. It was marked PRIVATE. ARTISTS ONLY. As he pushed the door open and passed through, he immediately found himself in an entirely different world. There were no red plush seats; everything was very bare. Lots of ropes hung down from the roof, pieces of scenery were stacked against the walls, and everyone seemed in a great hurry. Normally Paddington would have been most interested in everything, but now he had a purposeful look on his face.

Seeing a man bending over some scenery, he walked over and tapped him on the shoulder. "Excuse me," he said. "Can you tell me where the man is?"

The scene hand went on working. "Man?" he said. "*What* man?"

"*The* man," said Paddington, patiently. "The nasty man."

"Oh, you mean Sir Sealy." The scene hand pointed towards a long corridor. "He's in his dressing-room. You'd better not go disturbing him 'cause he's not in a very good mood." He looked up. "Hey!" he cried. "You're not supposed to be in here. Who let you in?"

Paddington was too far away to answer even if he had heard. He was already half-way up the corridor, looking closely at all the doors. Eventually he came to one with a large star on it

and the words SIR SEALY BLOOM in big gold
letters. Paddington drew a deep breath and then
knocked loudly. There was no reply, so he knocked
again. Still there was no reply, and so, very
cautiously, he pushed open the door with his paw.

"Go away!" said a booming voice. "I don't want
to see anyone."

Paddington peered round the door. Sir Sealy
Bloom was lying stretched out on a long couch.
He looked tired and cross. He opened one eye and
gazed at Paddington.

"I'm not signing any autographs," he growled.

"I don't want your autograph," said Paddington,
fixing him with a hard stare. "I wouldn't want your
autograph if I had my autograph book, and I
haven't got my autograph book so there!"

Sir Sealy sat up. "You don't want my autograph?"
he said, in a surprised voice. "But everyone always
wants my autograph!"

"Well, I don't," said Paddington. "I've come to
tell you to take your daughter back!" He gulped
the last few words. The great man seemed to have
grown to about twice the size he had been on the

stage, and he looked as if he was going to explode at any minute.

Sir Sealy clutched his forehead. "You want me to take my daughter back?" he said at last.

"That's right," said Paddington, firmly. "And if you don't, I expect she can come and stay with Mr and Mrs Brown."

Sir Sealy Bloom ran his hand distractedly through his hair and then pinched himself. "Mr and Mrs *Brown*," he repeated in a dazed voice. He looked wildly round the room and then dashed to the door. "Sarah!" he called, in a loud voice. "Sarah, come in here at once!" He backed round the room until he had placed the couch between himself and Paddington. "Keep away, bear!" he said, dramatically, and then peered at Paddington, for he was rather short-sighted. "You are a bear, aren't you?" he added.

"That's right," said Paddington. "From Darkest Peru!"

Sir Sealy looked at his woollen hat. "Well then," he said crossly, playing for time, "you ought to know better than to wear a green hat in my dressing-room. Don't you know green is a very unlucky colour in the theatre? Take it off at once."

"It's not my fault," said Paddington. "I wanted to wear my proper hat." He had just started to explain all about his hat when the door burst open and the lady called Sarah entered. Paddington immediately recognised her as Sir Sealy's daughter in the play.

"It's all right," he said. "I've come to rescue you."

"You've *what*?" The lady seemed most surprised.

"Sarah," Sir Sealy Bloom came out from behind the couch. "Sarah, protect me from this… this mad bear!"

"I'm not mad," said Paddington, indignantly.

"Then kindly explain what you are doing in my dressing-room," boomed the great actor.

Paddington sighed. Sometimes people were very slow to understand things. Patiently he explained it all to them. When he had finished, the lady called Sarah threw back her head and laughed.

"I'm glad you think it's funny," said Sir Sealy.

"But darling, don't you see?" she said. "It's a great compliment. Paddington really believes you were throwing me out into the world without a penny. It shows what a great actor you are!"

Sir Sealy thought for a moment. "Humph!" he said, gruffly. "Quite an understandable mistake, I suppose. He looks a remarkably intelligent bear, come to think of it."

Paddington looked from one to the other. "Then you were only acting all the time," he faltered.

The lady bent down and took his paw. "Of course, darling. But it was very kind of you to come to my rescue. I shall always remember it."

"Well, I *would* have rescued you if you'd wanted it," said Paddington.

Sir Sealy coughed. "Are you interested in the theatre, bear?" he boomed.

"Oh, yes," said Paddington. "Very much. Except I don't like having to pay so much for everything. I want to be an actor when I grow up."

The lady called Sarah jumped up. "Why, Sealy darling," she said, looking at Paddington. "I've an idea!" She whispered in Sir Sealy's ear and then Sir Sealy looked at Paddington. "It's a bit unusual," he said, thoughtfully. "But it's worth a try. Yes, it's certainly worth a try!"

In the theatre itself the interval was almost at an end and the Browns were getting restless.

"Oh, dear," said Mrs Brown. "I wonder where he's got to?"

"If he doesn't hurry up," said Mr Brown, "he's going to miss the start of the second act."

Just then there was a knock at the door and an attendant handed him a note. "A young bear gentleman asked me to give you this," he announced. "He said it was very urgent."

"Er… thank you," said Mr Brown, taking the note and opening it.

"What does it say?" asked Mrs Brown, anxiously. "Is he all right?"

Mr Brown handed her the note to read. "Your guess is as good as mine," he said.

Mrs Brown looked at it. It was hastily written in pencil and it said: I HAVE BEEN GIVEN A VERRY IMPORTANT JOB. PADINGTUN. P.S. I WILL TEL YOU ABOUT IT LAYTER.

"Now what on earth can that mean?" she said. "Trust something unusual to happen to Paddington."

"I don't know," said Mr Brown, settling back in

his chair as the lights went down. "But I'm not going to let it spoil the play."

"I hope the second half is better than the first," said Jonathan. "I thought the first half was rotten. That man kept on forgetting his lines."

The second half *was* much better than the first. From the moment Sir Sealy strode on to the stage the theatre was electrified. A great change had come over him. He no longer fumbled over his lines, and people who had coughed all through the first half now sat up in their seats and hung on his every word.

When the curtain finally came down on the end of the play, with Sir Sealy's daughter returning to his arms, there was a great burst of applause. The curtain rose again and the whole company bowed to the audience. Then it rose while Sir Sealy and Sarah bowed, but still the cheering went on. Finally Sir Sealy stepped forward and raised his hand for quiet.

"Ladies and gentlemen," he said. "Thank you for your kind applause. We are indeed most grateful. But before you leave I would like to introduce the youngest and most important member of our company. A young... er, bear, who came to our rescue..." The rest of Sir Sealy's speech was drowned in a buzz of excitement as he stepped forward to the very front of the stage, where a small screen hid a hole in the boards which was the prompt box.

He took hold of one of Paddington's paws and pulled. Paddington's head appeared through the hole. In his other paw he was grasping a copy of the script.

"Come along, Paddington," said Sir Sealy. "Come and take your bow."

"I can't," gasped Paddington. "I think I'm stuck!"

And stuck he was. It took several stagehands, the fireman, and a lot of butter to remove him after the audience had gone. But he was far enough out to twist round and raise his hat to the cheering crowd before the curtain came down for the last time.

Several nights later, anyone going into Paddington's room would have found him sitting up in bed with his scrapbook, a pair of scissors, and a pot of paste. He was busy pasting in a picture of Sir Sealy Bloom, which the great man had signed: 'To Paddington, with grateful thanks.' There was also a signed picture from the lady called Sarah, and one of his proudest possessions – a newspaper cutting about the play headed PADDINGTON SAVES THE DAY!

Mr Gruber had told him that the photographs were probably worth a bit of money, but after much thought he had decided not to part with them. In any case, Sir Sealy Bloom had given him his twenty pence back *and* a pair of opera glasses.

Chapter Seven

ADVENTURE AT THE SEASIDE

ONE MORNING MR Brown tapped the barometer in the hall. "It looks as if it's going to be a nice day," he said. "How about a trip to the sea?"

His remark was greeted with enthusiasm by the rest of the family, and in no time at all the house was in an uproar.

Mrs Bird started to cut a huge pile of sandwiches

while Mr Brown got the car ready. Jonathan and Judy searched for their bathing suits and Paddington went up to his room to pack. An outing which involved Paddington was always rather a business, as he insisted on taking all his things with him. As time went by he had acquired lots of things. As well as his suitcase, he now had a smart weekend grip with the initials P.B. inscribed on the side and a paper carrier-bag for the odds and ends.

For the summer months Mrs Brown had bought him a sun hat. It was made of straw and very floppy. Paddington liked it, for by turning the brim up or down, he could make it different shapes, and it was really like having several hats in one.

"When we get to Brightsea," said Mrs Brown, "we'll buy you a bucket and spade. Then you can make a sand-castle."

"And you can go to the pier," said Jonathan, eagerly. "They've some super machines on the pier. You'd better bring plenty of coins."

"And we can go swimming," added Judy. "You *can* swim, can't you?"

"Not very well, I'm afraid," replied Paddington. "You see, I've never been to the seaside before!"

"*Never* been to the seaside!" Everyone stopped what they were doing and stared at Paddington.

"Never," said Paddington.

They all agreed that it must be nice to be going to the seaside for the first time in one's life; even Mrs Bird began talking about the time she first went to Brightsea, many years before. Paddington became very excited as they told him all about the wonderful things he was going to see.

The car was crowded when they started off. Mrs Bird, Judy, and Jonathan sat in the back. Mr Brown drove and Mrs Brown and Paddington sat beside him. Paddington liked sitting in the front, especially when the window was open, so that he could poke his head out in the cool breeze. After a minor delay when Paddington's hat blew off on the outskirts of London, they were soon on the open road.

"Can you smell the sea yet, Paddington?" asked Mrs Brown after a while.

Paddington poked his head out and sniffed. "I can smell something," he said.

"Well," said Mr Brown. "Keep on sniffing, because we're almost there." And sure enough, as they reached the top of a hill and rounded a corner to go down the other side, there it was in the distance, glistening in the morning sun.

Paddington's eyes opened wide. "Look at all the boats on the dirt!" he cried, pointing in the direction of the beach with his paw.

Everyone laughed. "That's not dirt," said Judy. "That's sand." By the time they had explained all about sand to Paddington they were in Brightsea itself, and driving along the front. Paddington looked at the sea rather doubtfully. The waves were much bigger than he had imagined. Not so big as the ones he'd seen on his journey to England, but quite large enough for a small bear.

Mr Brown stopped the car by a shop on the esplanade and took out some money. "I'd like to fit this bear out for a day at the seaside," he said to the lady behind the counter. "Let's see now, we shall need a bucket and spade, a pair of sunglasses, one of those rubber tyres..." As he reeled off the list, the lady handed the articles to Paddington, who began to wish he had more than two paws. He had a rubber tyre round his middle which kept slipping down around his knees, a pair of sunglasses perched precariously on his nose, his straw hat, a bucket and spade in one hand, and his suitcase in the other.

"Photograph, sir?" Paddington turned to see an untidy man with a camera looking at him. "Only one pound, sir. Results guaranteed. Money back if you're not satisfied."

Paddington considered the matter for a moment. He didn't like the look of the man very much, but he had been saving hard for several weeks and now had just over three pounds. It would be nice to have a picture of himself.

"Won't take a minute, sir," said the man, disappearing behind a black cloth at the back of the camera. "Just watch the birdie."

Paddington looked around. There was no bird in sight as far as he could see. He went round behind the man and tapped him. The photographer, who appeared to be looking for something, jumped and then emerged from under his cloth. "How do you expect me to take your picture if you don't stand in front?" he asked in an aggrieved voice. "Now I've wasted a plate, and" – he looked shiftily at Paddington – "that will cost you one pound!"

Paddington gave him a hard stare. "You said there was a bird," he said. "And there wasn't."

"I expect it flew away when it saw your face," said the man nastily. "Now where's my pound?"

Paddington looked at him even harder for a moment. "Perhaps the bird took it when it flew away," he said.

"Ha! Ha! Ha!" cried another photographer, who had been watching the proceedings with interest. "Fancy you being taken in by a bear, Charlie! Serves you right for trying to take photographs without a licence. Now be off with you before I call a policeman."

He watched while the other man gathered up his belongings and slouched off in the direction of the pier, then he turned to Paddington. "These people are a nuisance," he said. "Taking away the living from honest folk. You did quite right not to pay him any money. And if you'll allow me, I'd like to take a nice picture of you myself, as a reward!"

The Brown family exchanged glances. "I don't know," said Mrs Brown. "Paddington always seems to fall on his feet."

"That's because he's a bear," said Mrs Bird darkly. "Bears always fall on their feet." She led the way on to the beach and carefully laid out a travelling rug on the sand behind a breakwater. "This will be as good a spot as any," she said. "Then we shall all know where to come back to, and no one will get lost."

"The tide's out," said Mr Brown. "So it will be nice and safe for bathing." He turned to Paddington. "Are you going in, Paddington?" he asked.

Paddington looked at the sea. "I might go for a paddle," he said.

"Well, hurry up," called Judy. "And bring your bucket and spade, then we can practise making sand-castles."

"Gosh!" Jonathan pointed to a notice pinned on the wall behind them. "Look… there's a sand-castle competition. Whizzo! First prize ten pounds for the biggest sand-castle!"

"Suppose we all join in and make one," said

Judy. "I bet the three of us together could make the biggest one you've ever seen."

"I don't think you're allowed to," said Mrs Brown, reading the notice. "It says here everyone has to make their own."

Judy looked disappointed. "Well, I shall have a go, anyway. Come on, you two, let's have a bathe first, then we can start digging after lunch." She raced down the sand closely followed by Jonathan and Paddington. At least, Jonathan followed but Paddington only got a few yards before his life-belt slipped down and he went headlong in the sand.

"Paddington, *do* give me your suitcase," called Mrs Brown. "You can't take it in the sea with you. It'll get wet and be ruined."

Looking rather crestfallen, Paddington handed his things to Mrs Brown for safekeeping and then ran down the beach after the others. Judy and Jonathan were already a long way out when he got there, so he contented himself with sitting on the water's edge for a while, letting the waves swirl around him as they came in. It was a nice feeling, a bit cold at first, but he soon got warm. He decided the seaside was a nice place to be. He paddled out to where the water was deeper and then lay back in his rubber tyre, letting the waves carry him gently back to the shore.

"Ten pounds! Supposing... supposing he won ten whole pounds!" He closed his eyes. In his mind he had a picture of a beautiful castle made of sand, like the one he'd once seen in a picture-book, with

battlements and towers and a moat. It was getting
bigger and bigger and everyone else on the beach
had stopped to gather round and cheer. Several
people said they had never seen such a big sand-
castle, and... he woke with a start as he felt
someone splashing water on him.

"Come on, Paddington," said Judy. "Lying there
in the sun fast asleep. It's time for lunch, and we've
got lots of work to do afterwards." Paddington felt
disappointed. It had been a nice sand-castle in his
dream. He was sure it would have won first prize.
He rubbed his eyes and followed Judy and Jonathan
up the beach to where Mrs Bird had laid out the
sandwiches – ham, egg, and cheese for everyone
else, and special marmalade ones for Paddington –
with ice-cream and fruit salad to follow.

"I vote," said Mr Brown, who had in mind an after-lunch nap for himself, "that after we've eaten you all go off in different directions and make your own sand-castles. Then we'll have our own private competition as well as the official one. I'll give a pound to the one with the biggest castle."

All three thought this was a good idea. "But don't go too far away," called Mrs Brown, as Jonathan, Judy and Paddington set off. "Remember the tide's coming in!" Her advice fell on deaf ears; they were all much too interested in sand-castles. Paddington especially was gripping his bucket and spade in a very determined fashion.

The beach was crowded and he had to walk quite a long way before he found a deserted spot. First of all he dug a big moat in a circle, leaving himself a drawbridge so that he could fetch and carry the sand for the castle itself. Then he set to work carrying bucketloads of sand to build the walls of the castle.

He was an industrious bear and even though it was hard work and his legs and paws soon got tired, he persevered until he had a huge pile of sand in the middle of his circle. Then he set to work with his spade, smoothing out the walls and making the battlements. They were very good battlements, with holes for windows and slots for the archers to fire through.

When he had finished he stuck his spade in one of the corner towers, placed his hat on top of that, and then lay down inside next to his marmalade jar and closed his eyes. He felt tired, but very pleased with himself. With the gentle roar of the sea in his ears he soon went fast asleep.

"We've been all along the beach," said Jonathan. "And we can't see him anywhere."

"He didn't even have his life-belt with him," said Mrs Brown anxiously. "Nothing. Just a bucket and spade." The Browns were gathered in a worried group round the man from the lifesaving hut.

"He's been gone several hours," said Mr Brown. "And the tide's been in over two!"

The man looked serious. "And you say he can't swim?" he asked.

"He doesn't even like having a bath much," said Judy. "So I'm sure he can't swim."

"Here's his photograph," said Mrs Bird. "He only had it taken this morning." She handed the man Paddington's picture and then dabbed her eyes with a handkerchief. "I know something's happened to him. He wouldn't have missed tea unless something was wrong."

The man looked at the picture. "We could send out a description," he said, dubiously. "But it's a job to see what he looks like by that. It's all hat and dark glasses."

"Can't you launch a lifeboat?" asked Jonathan, hopefully.

"We could," said the man. "If we knew where to look. But he might be anywhere."

"Oh, dear," Mrs Brown reached for her

handkerchief as well. "I can't bear to think about it."

"Something will turn up," said Mrs Bird, comfortingly. "He's got a good head on his shoulders."

"Well," said the man, holding up a dripping straw hat. "You'd better have this, and in the meantime… we'll see what we can do."

"There, there, Mary!" Mr Brown held his wife's arm. "Perhaps he just left it on the beach or something. It may have got picked up by the tide." He bent down to pick up the rest of Paddington's belongings. They seemed very small and lonely, lying there on their own.

"It's Paddington's hat all right," said Judy, examining it. "Look – it's got his mark inside!" She turned the hat inside out and showed them the outline of a paw mark in black ink and the words MY HAT – PADINGTUN.

"I vote we all separate," said Jonathan, "and comb the beach. We'll stand more chance that way."

Mr Brown looked dubious. "It's getting dark," he said.

Mrs Bird put down the travelling rug and folded her arms. "Well, I'm not going back until he's found," she said. "I couldn't go back to that empty house – not without Paddington."

"No one's thinking of going back without him, Mrs Bird," said Mr Brown. He looked helplessly out to sea. "It's just…"

"P'raps he didn't get swep' out to sea," said the lifesaving man, helpfully. "P'raps he's just gone on the pier or something. There seems to be a big crowd heading that way. Must be something interesting going on." He called out to a man who was just passing. "What's going on at the pier, chum?"

Without stopping, the man looked back over his shoulder and shouted, "Chap just crossed the Atlantic all by 'isself on a raft. 'Undreds of days without food or water so they say!" He hurried on.

The lifesaving man looked disappointed. "Another of these publicity stunts," he said. "We get 'em every year."

Mr Brown looked thoughtful. "I wonder," he said, looking in the direction of the pier.

"It would be just like him," said Mrs Bird. "It's the sort of thing that would happen to Paddington."

"It's got to be!" cried Jonathan. "It's just got to be!"

They all looked at each other and then, picking up their belongings, joined the crowd hurrying in the direction of the pier. It took them a long time to force their way through the turnstile, for the news that 'something was happening on the pier' had spread and there was a great throng at the entrance. But eventually, after Mr Brown had spoken to a policeman, a way was made for them and they were escorted to the very end, where the paddle-steamers normally tied up.

A strange sight met their eyes. Paddington, who had just been pulled out of the water by a fisherman, was sitting on his upturned bucket talking to some reporters. Several of them were taking photographs while the rest fired questions at him.

"Have you come all the way from America?" asked one reporter.

The Browns, hardly knowing whether to laugh or cry, waited eagerly for Paddington's reply.

"Well, no," said Paddington, truthfully, after a moment's pause. "Not America. But I've come a long way." He waved a paw vaguely in the direction of the sea. "I got caught by the tide, you know."

"And you sat in that bucket all the time?" asked another man, taking a picture.

"That's right," replied Paddington. "And I used my spade as a paddle. It was lucky I had it with me."

"Did you live on plankton?" queried another voice.

Paddington looked puzzled. "No," he said. "Marmalade."

Mr Brown pushed his way through the crowd. Paddington jumped up and looked rather guilty.

"Now then," said Mr Brown, taking his paw. "That's enough questions for today. This bear's been at sea for a long time and he's tired. In fact," he looked meaningfully at Paddington, "he's been at sea all the afternoon!"

"Is it still only Tuesday?" asked Paddington, innocently. "I thought it was much later than that!"

"Tuesday," said Mr Brown firmly. "And we've been worried to death over you!"

Paddington picked up his bucket and spade and jar of marmalade. "Well," he said. "I bet not many bears have gone to sea in a bucket, all the same."

It was dark when they drove along Brightsea front on their way home. The promenade was festooned with coloured lights and even the fountains in the gardens kept changing colour. It all looked very pretty. But Paddington, who was lying in the back of the car wrapped in a blanket, was thinking of his sand-castle.

"I bet mine was bigger than anyone else's," he said, sleepily.

"Bet you mine was the biggest," said Jonathan.

"I think," said Mr Brown, hastily, "you'd all better have a pound just to make sure."

"Perhaps we can come again another day," said Mrs Brown. "Then we can have another competition. How about that, Paddington?"

There was no reply from the back of the car. Sand-castles, paddling his bucket all across the harbour, and the sea air had proved too much for Paddington. He was fast asleep.

Chapter Eight

A DISAPPEARING TRICK

"OOOH," SAID PADDINGTON, "is it really for me?"
He stared hungrily at the cake. It really was a
wonderful cake. One of Mrs Bird's best. It was
covered with sugar icing and it had a cream and
marmalade filling. On the top there was one
candle and the words: TO PADDINGTON. WITH BEST
WISHES FOR A HAPPY BIRTHDAY – FROM EVERYONE.

It had been Mrs Bird's idea to have a birthday party. Paddington had been with them for two months. No one, not even Paddington, knew quite how old he was, so they decided to start again and call him one. Paddington thought this was a good idea, especially when he was told that bears had two birthdays every year – one in the summer and one in the winter.

"Just like the Queen," said Mrs Bird. "So you ought to consider yourself very important."

Paddington did. In fact, he went round to Mr Gruber straight away and told him the good news. Mr Gruber looked impressed and was pleased when Paddington invited him to the party.

"It's not often anyone invites me out, Mr Brown," he said. "I don't know when I went out last and I shall look forward to it very much indeed."

He didn't say any more at the time, but the next morning a van drew up outside the Browns' house and delivered a mysterious-looking parcel from all the shopkeepers in the Portobello Market.

"Aren't you a lucky bear," exclaimed Mrs Brown, when they opened the parcel and saw what was inside. It was a nice new shopping basket on wheels, with a bell on the side that Paddington could ring to let people know he was coming.

Paddington scratched his head. "It's a job to know what to do first," he said, as he carefully placed the basket with the other presents. "I shall have a lot of 'thank you' letters to write."

"Perhaps you'd better leave them until tomorrow," said Mrs Brown hastily. Whenever Paddington wrote any letters he generally managed to get more ink on himself than on the paper, and he was looking so unusually smart, having had a bath the night before, that it seemed a pity to spoil it.

Paddington looked disappointed. He liked writing letters. "Perhaps I can help Mrs Bird in the kitchen," he said hopefully.

"I'm glad to say," said Mrs Bird, as she emerged from the kitchen, "that I've just finished. But you can lick the spoon if you like." She had bitter memories of other occasions when Paddington had 'helped' in the kitchen. "But not too much," she warned, "or you won't have room for this."

It was then that Paddington saw his cake for the

first time. His eyes, usually large and round, became so much larger and rounder, that even Mrs Bird blushed with pride. "Special occasions demand special things," she said, and hurried off in the direction of the dining-room.

Paddington spent the rest of the day being hurried from one part of the house to another as preparations were made for his party. Mrs Brown was busy tidying up. Mrs Bird was busy in the kitchen. Jonathan and Judy were busy with the decorations. Everyone had a job except Paddington.

"I thought it was supposed to be *my* birthday," he grumbled, as he was sent packing into the drawing-room for the fifth time after upsetting a box of marbles over the kitchen floor.

"So it is, dear," said a flustered Mrs Brown. "But your time comes later." She was beginning to regret telling him that bears had two birthdays every year, for already he was worrying about when the next one was due.

"Now just you watch out of the window for the postman," she said, lifting him up on to the window-sill. But Paddington didn't seem very keen on this. "Or else," she said, "practise doing some of your conjuring tricks, ready for this evening."

Among Paddington's many presents was a conjuring outfit from Mr and Mrs Brown. It was a very expensive one from Barkridges. It had a special magic table, a large mystery box which made things disappear if you followed the instructions properly, a magic wand and several packs of cards. Paddington emptied them all over the floor and settled down in the middle to read the book of instructions.

He sat there for a long time, studying the pictures and diagrams, and reading everything twice to make sure. Every now and then he absent-mindedly dipped a paw into his marmalade pot, and then, remembering it was his birthday and that there was a big tea to come, he reached up and stood the jar on the magic table before returning to his studies.

The first chapter was called SPELLS. It showed how to wave the magic wand and the correct way to say

ABRACADABRA. Paddington stood up clutching the book in one paw, and waved the wand several times through the air. He also tried saying ABRACADABRA. He looked round. Nothing seemed to have changed, and he was just about to try again, when his eyes nearly popped out of his head. The jar of marmalade which he'd placed on the magic table only a few minutes before had disappeared!

He searched hurriedly through the book. There was nothing about making marmalade disappear. Worse still, there was nothing about making it come back again, either. Paddington decided it must be a very powerful spell to make a whole pot vanish into thin air.

He was about to rush outside and tell the others when he thought better of it. It might be a good trick to do in the evening, especially if he could persuade Mrs Bird to give him another jar. He went out into the kitchen and waved his wand a few times in Mrs Bird's direction, just to make sure.

"I'll give you ABRACADABRA," said Mrs Bird, pushing him out again. "And be careful with that stick or you'll have someone's eye out."

Paddington returned to the drawing-room and tried saying his spell backwards. Nothing happened, so he started reading the next chapter of the instruction book, which was called THE MYSTERY OF THE DISAPPEARING EGG.

"I shouldn't have thought you needed any book to tell you that," said Mrs Bird at lunch time, as Paddington told them all about it. "The way you gobble your food is nobody's business."

"Well," said Mr Brown, "so long as you don't try sawing anyone in half this evening, I don't mind."

"I was only joking," he added hurriedly, as Paddington turned an inquiring gaze on him. Nevertheless, as soon as lunch was over, Mr Brown hurried down the garden and locked up his tools. With Paddington there was no sense in taking chances.

As it happened he had no cause to worry, for Paddington had far too many things on his mind what with one thing and another. The whole family was there for tea as well as Mr Gruber. Several other people came along too, including the Browns' next door neighbour, Mr Curry. The last named was a most unwelcome visitor. "Just because there's a free tea," said Mrs Bird. "I think it's disgusting, taking the crumbs off a young bear's plate like that. He's not even been invited!"

"He'll have to look slippy if he gets any crumbs off Paddington's plate," said Mr Brown. "All the same, it *is* a bit thick, after all the things he's said in the past. And not even bothering to wish him many happy returns."

Mr Curry had a reputation in the neighbourhood for meanness and for poking his nose into other people's business. He was also very bad-tempered, and was always complaining about the least little thing which met with his disapproval. In the past that had often included Paddington, which was why the Browns had not invited him to the party.

But even Mr Curry had no cause to complain about the tea. From the huge birthday cake down to the last marmalade sandwich, everyone voted it was the best tea they had ever had. Paddington himself was so full he had great difficulty in mustering enough breath to blow out the candle. But at last he managed it without singeing his whiskers, and everyone, including Mr Curry, applauded and wished him a happy birthday.

"And now," said Mr Brown, when the noise had died down. "If you'll all move your seats back, I think Paddington has a surprise for us."

While everyone was busy moving their seats to one side of the room, Paddington disappeared into the drawing-room and returned carrying his conjuring outfit. There was a short delay while he erected his magic table and adjusted the mystery box, but soon all was ready. The lights were turned off except for a standard lamp and Paddington waved his wand for quiet.

"Ladies and gentlemen," he began, consulting his instruction book, "my next trick is impossible!"

"But you haven't done one yet," grumbled Mr Curry.

Ignoring the remark, Paddington turned over the page. "For this trick," he said, "I shall require an egg."

"Oh dear," said Mrs Bird, as she hurried out to the kitchen, "I know something dreadful is going to happen."

Paddington placed the egg in the centre of his magic table and covered it with a handkerchief. He muttered ABRACADABRA several times and then hit the handkerchief with his wand.

Mr and Mrs Brown looked at each other. They were both thinking of their carpet. "Hey presto!" said Paddington, and pulled the handkerchief away. To everyone's surprise the egg had completely disappeared.

"Of course," said Mr Curry, knowledgeably, above the applause, "it's all done by sleight of paw. But very good though, for a bear. Very good indeed. Now make it come back again!"

Feeling very pleased with himself, Paddington took his bow and then felt in the secret compartment behind the table. To his surprise he found something much larger than an egg. In fact... it was a jar of marmalade. It was the one that had disappeared that very morning! He displayed it in his paw; the applause for this trick was even louder.

"Excellent," said Mr Curry, slapping his knee. "Making people think he was going to find an egg, and it was a jar of marmalade all the time. Very good indeed!"

Paddington turned over a page. "And now," he announced, flushed with success, "the disappearing trick!" He took a bowl of Mrs Brown's best flowers and placed them on the dining-table alongside his mystery box. He wasn't very happy about this trick, as he hadn't had time to practise it, and he wasn't at all sure how the mystery box worked or even where you put the flowers to make them disappear.

He opened the door in the back of the box and then poked his head round the side. "I shan't be a minute," he said, and then disappeared from view again.

The audience sat in silence. "Rather a slow trick, this one," said Mr Curry, after a while.

"I hope he's all right," said Mrs Brown. "He seems very quiet."

"Well, he can't have gone far," said Mr Curry. "Let's try knocking." He got up, knocked loudly on the box, and then put his ear to it. "I can hear someone calling," he said. "It sounds like Paddington. I'll try again." He shook the box and there was an answering thump from inside.

"I think he's shut himself in," said Mr Gruber. He too knocked on the box and called out, "Are you all right, Mr Brown?"

"NO!" said a small and muffled voice. "It's dark and I can't read my instruction book."

"Quite a good trick," said Mr Curry, some while later after they had prised open Paddington's mystery box with a penknife. He helped himself to some biscuits. "The disappearing bear. Very unusual! But I still don't see what the flowers were for."

Paddington looked at him suspiciously, but Mr Curry was far too busy with the biscuits.

"For my next trick," said Paddington, "I would like a watch."

"Are you sure?" asked Mrs Brown, anxiously. "Wouldn't anything else do?"

Paddington consulted his instruction book. "It says a watch," he said, firmly.

Mr Brown hurriedly pulled his sleeve down over his left wrist. Unfortunately, Mr Curry, who was in an unusually good mood after his free tea, stood up and offered his. Paddington took it gratefully and placed it on the table. "This is a jolly good trick," he said, reaching down into his box and pulling out a small hammer.

He covered the watch with a handkerchief and then hit it several times. Mr Curry's expression froze. "I hope you know what you're doing, young bear," he said.

Paddington looked rather worried. Having turned over the page he'd just read the ominous words, "It is necessary to have a second watch for this trick." Gingerly, he lifted up a corner of the handkerchief. Several cogs and some pieces of glass rolled across the table. Mr Curry let out a roar of wrath.

"I think I forgot to say ABRACADABRA," faltered Paddington.

"ABRACADABRA!" shouted Mr Curry, beside himself with rage. "ABRACADABRA!" He held up the remains of his watch. "Twenty years I've had this watch, and now look at it! This will cost someone a pretty penny!"

Mr Gruber took out an eyeglass and examined the watch carefully. "Nonsense," he said, coming to Paddington's rescue. "It's one you bought from me for three pounds six months ago! You ought to be ashamed of yourself, telling lies in front of a young bear!"

"Rubbish!" spluttered Mr Curry. He sat down heavily on Paddington's chair. "Rubbish! I'll give you…" his voice trailed away and a peculiar expression came over his face. "I'm sitting on something," he said. "Something wet and sticky!"

"Oh dear," said Paddington. "I expect it's my disappearing egg. It must have reappeared!"

Mr Curry grew purple in the face. "I've never been so insulted in my life," he said. "Never!" He turned at the door and waved an accusing finger at the company. "It's the last time I shall ever come to one of *your* birthday parties!"

"Henry," said Mrs Brown, as the door closed behind Mr Curry, "you really oughtn't to laugh."

Mr Brown tried hard to keep a straight face. "It's no good," he said, bursting out. "I can't help it."

"Did you see his face when all the cogs rolled out?" said Mr Gruber, his face wet with tears.

"All the same," said Mr Brown, when the laughter had died down. "I think perhaps you ought to try something a little less dangerous next time, Paddington."

"How about that card trick you were telling me about, Mr Brown?" asked Mr Gruber. "The one where you tear up a card and make it come out of someone's ear."

"Yes, that sounds a nice quiet one," said Mrs Brown. "Let's see that."

"You wouldn't like another disappearing trick?" asked Paddington, hopefully.

"Quite sure, dear," said Mrs Brown.

"Well," said Paddington, rummaging in his box, "it's not very easy doing card tricks when you've only got paws, but I don't mind trying."

He offered a pack of cards to Mr Gruber, who

solemnly took one from the middle and then memorised it before replacing the card. Paddington waved his wand over the pack several times and then withdrew a card. He held up the seven of spades. "Was this it?" he said to Mr Gruber.

Mr Gruber polished his glasses and stared. "You know," he said, "I do believe it was!"

"I bet all the cards are the same," whispered Mr Brown to his wife.

"Ssh!" said Mrs Brown. "I thought he did it very well."

"This is the difficult bit," said Paddington, tearing it up. "I'm not very sure about this part." He put the pieces under his handkerchief and tapped them several times with the wand.

"Oh!" said Mr Gruber, rubbing the side of his head. "I felt something go pop in my ear just then. Something cold and hard." He felt in his ear. "Why I do believe…" He held up a shining round object to the audience. "It's a sovereign! My birthday present for Paddington! Now I wonder how it got in there?"

"Oooh!" said Paddington, as he proudly examined it. "I didn't expect that. Thank you very much, Mr Gruber."

"Well," said Mr Gruber. "It's only a small present I'm afraid, Mr Brown. But I've enjoyed the little chats we've had in the mornings. I look forward to them very much and, er," he cleared his throat and looked around, "I'm sure we all hope you have many more birthdays!"

When the chorus of agreement had died down, Mr Brown rose and looked at the clock. "And now," he said, "it's long past all our bedtimes, most of all yours, Paddington, so I suggest we all do a disappearing trick now."

"I wish," said Paddington, as he stood at the door waving everyone goodbye, "I wish my Aunt Lucy could see me now. She'd feel very pleased."

"You'll have to write and tell her all about it, Paddington," said Mrs Brown, as she took his paw. "But in the morning," she added hastily. "You've got clean sheets, remember."

"Yes," said Paddington. "In the morning. I expect if I did it now I'd get ink over the sheets or something. Things are always happening to me."

"You know, Henry," said Mrs Brown, as they watched Paddington go up the stairs to bed, looking rather sticky and more than a little sleepy, "it's nice having a bear about the house."

Postscript

A Bear Called Paddington didn't begin life as a book. The opening paragraph was simply an early-morning doodle brought on by the certain knowledge that if I didn't put something down on the blank sheet of paper in my typewriter nobody else would.

However, it caught my fancy, so I wrote a second paragraph, then a third, until by the end of the day I had completed a whole story.

The source of my inspiration was a toy bear sitting on the mantelpiece of our one-room flat near London's Portobello market. I had bought it in desperation the previous Christmas Eve as a stocking-filler for my wife, and we called him Paddington because I had always liked the sound of it and names are important, particularly if you are a bear and don't have very much else in the world.

In no time at all he became part of the family. In fact, for a long time he *was* the family and was treated as such; joining us at meal times, sharing our holidays, occasionally interrupting our conversations.

Ten working days later, having completed seven more stories, I realised I had a book on my hands. It hadn't been written with any particular age group in mind, which was fortunate, because until then I had always written for adults and if I had consciously aimed at a young audience I might have 'written down', which is always a bad idea. Anyway, I agree with Gertrude Stein: a book is a book is a book, and it should be enjoyable on all levels.

It was lucky, too, that I picked on a bear for my doodling. The late Peter Bull, actor and arctophile, once said that whereas dolls are always wondering what they are going to wear next, you never know quite what bears are thinking, and he was right. You feel you can trust them with your secrets and they won't pass them on. Another thing about bears is that one perceives them in the wild lumbering around on two legs, so they are already halfway to being human.

The first book in a series is always the most fun to write. The world is your oyster and you can go wherever your fancy takes you. However, at the same time you build in certain parameters which are there for all time. Although Paddington's adventures take place in the present, I always picture him going home at the end of the day to the rather safer pre-war world which I remember from my childhood.

I don't think they ever realised it, but my parents served as role models for Mr and Mrs Brown. (There is also a lot of my father in Paddington, for he was very law-abiding and never went out without a hat in case he bumped into someone he knew and had nothing to raise.) Jonathan and Judy were there to bridge the age gap. Mrs Bird was based on memories of my childhood best friend's live-in nanny. Paddington's 'best friend', Mr Gruber, is important because he knows what it is like to be a refugee in a strange country, so they have a special relationship. The Browns' long-suffering next-door neighbour, Mr Curry, triggers off many a story. I have only to put the two together and things start to happen. 'Number 32 Windsor Gardens' I saw as being just around the corner from our flat.

Paddington was, and always will be, very real to me. He has his feet firmly on the ground and he has a very strong sense of right and wrong. So much so that when I come up against a problem in my own life I often ask myself what he would do.

The fact that others believe in him just as much is rewarding. For example, the boy who wrote saying he was so used to Paddington being the name of a bear it now seemed a funny name for a station. And the nun who wrote to me out of the blue telling me she was in hospital – I suspect suffering from an incurable disease – and thanking me for all the comfort Paddington brought her. He couldn't have had a greater compliment paid him.

Writing comedy is a serious business; a matter of distillation, of finding exactly the right word. On the whole, without the benefit of an immediate audience response, one works in a kind of vacuum.

However, I did once find myself sitting in a restaurant and overhearing two men in the next booth discussing Paddington's exploits. They were both laughing their heads off, and that was very satisfying because in the circumstances it was obviously genuine. I didn't let on I was there for fear of embarrassing both parties.

Then, some years ago, on a promotional tour in

Australia, I had to carry a stuffed Paddington everywhere I went. Each time I boarded a plane I knew it wouldn't be long before he would be asked up to the flight deck. On one occasion I left him up there, strapped into a spare bucket seat while the crew explained the controls. A little later on I received a second message asking if I would mind him staying up there because he wanted to practise landing the plane. I didn't tell the other passengers!

When I wrote the first book I had no idea that he would eventually be honoured with a life-size bronze statue on the station itself. People use the plinth to sit on while they eat their sandwiches, which is rather apposite really, and it's nice to think they will probably still be doing it long after I have gone.

I don't suppose we shall ever meet, but if we do I shan't be at all surprised. Being a polite bear I'm sure he will raise his hat, and as we go our separate ways I shall regret not wearing one too, so that I could raise it in return as a mark of respect.

MICHAEL BOND

April 2001

MORE THAN A STORY

Contents Page

THE BEAR FACTS

There are many species and sub-species of bears including the **Brown Bear**, the **Polar Bear**, the **Sloth Bear**, the **Giant Panda** and the **Spectacle Bear**, but thanks to his Aunt Lucy, Paddington is the only one who speaks good English!

Bears in the wild can be very fierce, especially if they feel threatened. The brown bear isn't called 'grizzly' for nothing and the polar bear is especially fierce, but Paddington finds his 'hard stare' beats all the others put together. He doesn't use it very often, but when he does… watch out!

Many bears are now in danger of extinction. Once there were over 100,000 grizzly bears in the USA but today there are fewer than 1,500.

Koalas are often referred to as bears due to their appearance; they are not bears, however, but marsupials.

Make your own Compass

In case you ever get lost in Darkest Peru, here's how to make a compass to help you find your way!

To make a very simple compass you will need:

- A horseshoe magnet
- A large needle (and an adult to help you with this)
- A small piece of cork
- Glue
- A bowl of water

Instructions:

Stroke the pointed end of the needle thirty or forty times over one end of the magnet.

Place it lengthwise and glue it across the middle of the cork.

Place the cork in the bowl, making sure the needle is above water.

The needle will swing in a North to South line, and either the pointed end of the 'eye' will be facing the North Pole.

You can tell which end of the needle is facing North, if you remember that the sun rises in the East, and if you face the North then East is always on your right.

MAP MAKING

Paddington is very keen on maps. He was once in trouble for drawing a map of South America on the bathroom floor with Mr Brown's shaving cream. A much less messy way of making a map is with a pencil and paper. Here's how to do it:

* Draw a map of the area where you live.

* Show your house and your street. Then include the houses of your friends and neighbours.

* Now draw the local parks, your school, local shops and any other important landmarks.

* When you've finished drawing the map, colour it.

* Use dark brown for the busy main roads and lighter brown for the smaller ones. Mark in any Pedestrian crossings.

* Colour the parks green and label all the streets and buildings.

* Carry the map with you, and if you ever get lost you can show it to a policeman and ask him to help you.

Remember: the top of the map should always face North. If you don't know where North is, use the compass you made over the page.

PADDINGTON STATION

* Paddington Railway Station is situated on Praed Street in London.

* The station's grand opening was on the 16th January 1854, having taken 4 years to build! It was built as the terminus (where the railway track stops) of the Great Western Railway.

* The station was built by Isambard Kingdom Brunel, assisted by the English architect Matthew Digby Wyatt, who helped him design it.

* Isambard Kingdom Brunel was a great Victorian English engineer who built twenty-five railways lines, over a hundred bridges and three ships. The last ship he built was called The Great Eastern and was the biggest ship in the world at that time.

* There is a statue of Brunel on the station concourse known as 'The Lawn'. (The concourse is the large open space before the ticket barriers where people wait before getting on their trains.)

* Today, Paddington Station has 14 terminal platforms and two underground tube train platforms.

* £63 million was recently spent on giving the station a new lease of life and a 'makeover', including new cafés and shops.

* If you are ever in Paddington Station, while you are there look out for Paddington Bear's very own statue made of bronze…

ONE OF PADDINGTON'S FAVOURITE RECIPES

Aunt Lucy's Layer Delight

Try making this delicious sweet which is served at the Home for Retired Bears in Lima on their annual Open Day Festival.

Serves two

Ingredients:

- a small carton of plain yoghurt
- an equal quantity of double cream (or crème fraîche for a healthier option)
- about 8 grapes, peeled and cut in half
- 2 tablespoons of brown sugar
- 2 glacé cherries

Here's how to make it:

Mix together the yoghurt and the double cream or crème fraîche.

Take one tall glass with straight sides for each person. Fill the glass with alternate layers of the cream and yoghurt mixture, the sliced grapes and brown sugar.

Top with a cherry. Chill in the fridge until ready to serve.

BRIGHTSEA SAND ART

Paddington decided to send his Aunt Lucy a postcard with a sand paw-mark on it using real Brightsea sand.

Why don't you have a go?

You will need:

- A plain postcard
- Glue or paste
- A paint brush
- Fine sand

What to do:

Dip your brush in the glue or paste mixture and paint a pattern on the card. At once cover the postcard with sand.

Shake off any loose sand.

You will be left with a sand-patterned postcard.

Remember to deliver your postcard by hand, as your postman won't be happy if his pillar box is full of sand!

MARMALADE MADNESS!

Q. What's square and white outside, orange inside,
and can travel at over 100 miles an hour?

A. A train-driver's marmalade sandwich!

- Paddington's Aunt Lucy says, 'A spoonful of marmalade a day keeps the doctor at bay,' and she should know. She's one of the oldest inhabitants of the Home for Retired Bears.

- In 2007, the world's most expensive marmalade was produced by F. Duerr & Son and it was valued at between £300 and £400. That's £76 per slice of marmalade covered toast!

- Another of Aunt Lucy's sayings is, 'It's a wise bear who knows where his next marmalade sandwich is coming from.' That's why Paddington never goes anywhere without having one under his hat.

- On the 18th February 2007, the world's first Marmalade Festival took place in Cumbria. The highlight was a marmalade tasting competition. With over 350 entries from all over the world, it took the judges almost 10 hours to taste them all. The festival is now an annual event.

A FEW MARMALADE **DOS** AND **DON'TS**

- If you keep a marmalade sandwich under your hat in case of an emergency, **do** be very careful when you raise it.

- If you take a book out of the library, **don't** use a chunk to mark something special.

- If you visit a maze, **do** make sure you leave a marmalade chunk every time you turn a corner. If you get lost you can always find your way out again and have a snack at the same time.

- On the other hand, if you get taken to the theatre and sit in the front row, **don't** leave a marmalade sandwich on the ledge in front of you. Paddington did and it fell on a man's head during an exciting part of the play!

A VERY MAGIC POSTCARD

Is it really possible to pass a bear through a postcard?

This trick has always been very popular at the Home for Retired Bears in Lima, and it was passed on to Paddington before he left for England.

If you hold up a postcard in front of your audience and say you will cut a hole in it large enough for someone to crawl through it, it sounds impossible!

The trick is in the way you cut the hole...

★ Be VERY CAREFUL with the scissors and get an adult to help you ★

1. Fold the card in half lengthways as shown.

2. Next, take a pair of scissors and make a series of cuts from the outer edge inwards, stopping short of the fold.

3. Follow this with a second series of cuts between the first row, starting from the folded edge and stopping short of the outer edge.

4. Finally, cut along the folded edge from point (a) to point (b), leaving the two outer folds intact.

The 'postcard' will now open out into a giant ring.

HOW WELL DO YOU KNOW PADDINGTON?

Take the quiz and find out! Choose the answer you think is correct, and count up your score at the end.

1. Paddington's favourite snack is:

a) toast and honey   b) chocolate pudding

c) marmalade sandwiches   d) treacle tart

2. The Browns first met Paddington:

a) on holiday in Peru   b) at the zoo

c) on the beach at Brightsea   d) outside the Lost Property office at Paddington Station

3. The Brown's housekeeper is called:

a) Mrs Fox   b) Mrs Bird

c) Mrs Bull   d) Mrs Finch

4. Paddington wears:

a) a mackintosh   b) a cape

c) a duffle coat   d) a parka

5. Paddington lives at:

a) 6 Portobello Road   b) 26 Victoria Place

c) 32 Windsor Gardens   d) 18 Railway Cuttings

6. Mr Brown:

a) is a stationmaster   b) works in the City

c) owns a bunshop   d) has a stall in the Portobello Market

7. Paddington's very first adventure at the Brown's home was with:

a) a lawnmower   b) a bath
c) a pan of toffee   d) a vacuum cleaner

8. How many birthdays does Paddington have each year?

a) 1   b) 2
c) 3   d) 4

9. Paddington's Aunt Lucy lives in:

a) Australia   b) England
c) Peru   d) Mexico

10. The Capital of Darkest Peru is:

a) Stow-On-The-Wold   b) Santiago
c) Lima   d) Brussels

Answers:
1: c); 2: d); 3: b); 4: c); 5: c);
6: b); 7: b); 8: b); 9: c); 10: c)

Score:
8-10:   Excellent! Give yourself a pat on the back!
5-7:   Fair. Keep reading about Paddington and you'll get top marks next time!
Under 5: You've obviously still got quite a few of Paddington's adventures to find out about!